CHRISTMAS OF NEW BEGINNINGS

Folk singer Cerys Davies left Wales for the South Downs village of Pad-cock at Christmas, desperate for a new beginning. And she ends up having plenty of those: opening a new craft shop and tea room, helping set up the village's first festive craft fair . . . and, of course, falling desperately in love with Lovely Sam, the owner of the local pub! Between mild espionage, festive magic, and a flock of pub-crashing sheep, could this Christmas lead to her best new beginning yet?

KIRSTY FERRY

CHRISTMAS OF NEW BEGINNINGS

Complete and Unabridged

LINFORD
Leicester

First published in Great Britain in 2021 by
Choc Lit Limited
Surrey

First Linford Edition
published 2022
by arrangement with
Choc Lit Limited
Surrey

*A catalogue record for this book is available
from the British Library.*

ISBN 978–1–4448–4970–7

Published by
Ulverscroft Limited
Anstey, Leicestershire

Printed and bound in Great Britain by
TJ Books Ltd., Padstow, Cornwall

This book is printed on acid-free paper

To my family with love.

Acknowledgements

Thank you for indulging me with a trip to another fictional village that popped into my head, along with its raft of slightly bonkers inhabitants. After the last couple of years, I really wanted to write a feel-good festive story, and I hope this one doesn't disappoint.

Padcock village, which is introduced here in *Christmas of New Beginnings*, is alive and buzzing in my head, and I can close my eyes and find myself walking down its streets and greeting the inhabitants like old friends. It's based very loosely on Lacock in Wiltshire, a village in the care of the National Trust and a famous filming location for films and TV shows such as *Harry Potter*, *Pride and Prejudice*, *Downton Abbey* — and, my favourite: the live-action version of Disney's *Beauty and the Beast*. Padcock Court is therefore based very loosely on Lacock Abbey: a stately home in the village which was home to Henry

Fox-Talbot, a scientist, inventor and photography pioneer. There is a very famous photograph Fox-Talbot took in August 1835 of a latticed window in the house, which is created from possibly the oldest existing camera negative — and to this day that latticed window is probably one of the most photographed areas of the house! Padcock Court is perhaps more of a smaller, slightly crumbling stately home, but the inspiration is definitely there.

I have to thank the wonderful Choc Lit and Ruby family for allowing my indulgence to become a published book, and as always, huge thanks to my lovely editor and my fabulous cover designer, and the Choc Lit Stars and Tasting Panel who helped to get the Padcock Series off my computer and out into the world. Special thanks to: Dimitra Evangelou, Emily Seldon, Jenny Kinsman, Liana Vera Saez, Lisa Vasil, Mel Appleyard, Ruth Nägele, Sharon Walsh, and Yvonne Greene.

And big, big thanks must go, as always,

to my family and also, this time, to my dog, Robbie. This book was written in the first lockdown of 2020, and supervised closely by the dog as he ensured I shared all my biscuits with him and slept on my feet for most of it.

And he was, it has to be said, very warm.

1

Christmas Present

(Okay, so it's a little bit before Christmas Present, but we'll get to that)

I'm quite used to sheep. I lived in Wales for much of my life, so the woolly little creatures — or, let's face it, big creatures because sheep *can* be surprisingly big — used to be part and parcel of my daily existence.

However, I don't think they're usually welcome in a pub.

The pub in question is the Spatchcock Inn in Padcock. Padcock is a village in the South Downs, and Padcock is now my home. It's one of those quaint little villages that are probably better recognised as the background to a costume drama rather than known in their own right, because the village is often used, well . . . as the background to a costume drama, and Padcock

Court, the big old manor house, has cropped up in more than one Jane Austen adaptation. It's all a question of clever camera angles, so the viewers don't guess that the same house plays the part of a parlour in Pemberley or a nook in Northanger Abbey. It's not unusual to see actors wandering around in all kinds of different costumes in Padcock. In fact, this particular year it's been quite special, because they've been filming a version of Dickens' *A Christmas Carol* in the village. The crew said if anyone was interested, we could be extras and drift around as townsfolk. I loved the idea of dressing up in pretty clothes and crinolines. So next year I'll be on TV — yay!

Sadly, by the time I got around to signing up to do it, the only roles they had left to fill were 'beggar woman' or 'pregnant pauper' — no doubt so they could put us in an old sack or some variation of rags and didn't have to fork out on a crinoline.

As a result, there I was a few weeks

before Christmas, sitting in the Spatch-cock and thoughtfully stroking my fake baby bump, clad in a brown piece of sack-ing and a dingy grey shawl, with a poke bonnet on my head. We'd wrapped up filming that day; it was all very exciting, and we'd decided a good way to unwind so close to Christmas was to hit the pub, have festive 'victuals' as Veronica from the WI had suggested, sing carols around the tree and see who could hog the seats next to the real log fire in the inglenook.

The reality was that people had decided they'd have drinks first, and beyond a *Now Christmas* CD that was playing on a loop, they didn't really have the facilities for carolling in the Spatch-cock — although I knew from experience that the acoustics were quite nice in the old building.

Drinking mulled wine and eating mince pies worked for me though. That was fine.

My best friend Edie was sitting next to me. She had declined the chance to be an extra — no doubt because she'd look weird in anything other than her usual 1960's styling, and she'd definitely have to take off her industrial-strength eyeliner and remove her chandelier ear-rings to participate.

Also, I don't think a loud, drunken, sweary beggar was what they were after.

Of course, I might be wrong there; I guess beggars may well have been loud, drunken and sweary but, nevertheless, Edie was loud, drunken and sweary in a twenty-first-century way, rather than a nineteenth-century way. At that precise moment, for instance, she was loudly and swearily complaining that her nem-esis, Ninian Chambers, had secured a Christmas art exhibition in London, and that it 'just wasn't fair, actually'. I zoned out. I'd heard endless rants about this particular man. Edie was an artist and had been quite successful until she'd lost her gran, who had basically brought her up. She'd sort of retreated to her gran's cottage in Padcock and lost her way a little. Currently, she worked part-time for me (although she would tell you it was 'with' me) in the village craft shop/ tea room, and provided a lot of stuff for the tourists — postcards and paintings of the village, that kind of thing. But I knew for a fact she kept one eye on London and another on Ninian Chambers. She also had a freelance graphic design business that was doing quite well.

It was this that I was pondering as I stroked my tummy. *If she's got one eye on London and one on Ninian, how many eyes does Edie actually have? Because she definitely also has one eye on the bottle of wine which is rapidly emptying in front of us . . .*

It was at that point that the sheep burst through the door.

At least the thundering of ovine hooves shut Edie up. As for me, I simply looked up, serene in my 'pregnancy', and saw the mass of wool and legs and very stupid faces tumble in. Sheep always *do* look a bit daft.

'Sheep look daft, don't they?' I commented as Edie screeched and jumped out of her seat. She kind of bounded behind me — she's a Londoner at heart, bless her — and trembled, huddling very close to the Christmas tree.

'Oh my God. What *are* they?'

'Sheep.'

'I know that! I mean what *are* they? Why are they *here*? What *purpose* do they have in Padcock?'

'I think they're extras for the filming.'

'Are there even sheep in *A Christmas Carol*?'

I shrugged. I didn't know. I just knew we'd finished filming for the day and I'd come straight here. I hadn't seen any sheep in the scenes I'd done though. Admittedly, I was basically just wandering around the street behind the main cast and stealing fruit from the Christmas market stalls as other people shook their fists at me in a blizzard of fake snow — even though some of the real stuff had been forecast, it hadn't decided to float down from the heavens just yet. Veronica, to be fair, had done a jolly good fist-shake. It was almost as if she meant it, looming out at me from behind her plywood barrel. I made a mental note to make as many cupcakes as I could muster for her summer fair so I didn't have to endure a *real* fist-shake from her.

'*Potentially*, there *are* sheep,' I said thoughtfully, gazing upon the seething tumult of woolly animals. 'There's a market scene. Scrooge may be bellowing at sheep to get out of the way — shepherds being poor people and all that.' I pulled a face.

'But there are *sheep*. In the *Spatchcock*!'

By now the place was in an uproar, and people were yelling about sheep and wild animals. I distinctly heard Veronica say something like 'keep it off my drink, keep it away!' and I shifted position slightly, wondering if I should get up and herd them out. We used to have a Border collie when I was a child, and I like to think it taught me a thing or two. In fact, for three years I genuinely thought I was a Border collie. I remember the dog was also very good at herding me and my brother to wherever we had to be at any particular time.

Then there was a shout from behind

the bar. 'Oh hell's bells! What are those things doing in my pub?' Sam, the owner of the Spatchcock, and also the most divine barman ever, had just come through from the snug and was standing behind the bar, his eyes wide and disbelieving. There was a crash as he slammed the tray he'd been carrying down, then leapt — he actually *leapt* — over the counter-top and ran towards the flock.

'Lovely Sam,' muttered a frenzied Edie. 'Lovely Sam will save us.'

Lovely Sam — it was his very apt nickname — plunged into the woolly mass, and was promptly swallowed up in it.

'Oh dear.' I pushed the chair back and stood up. 'Lovely Sam runs the risk of being squashed.'

I waddled — it was a pretty convincing costume, I had to say — towards the melee and waved my arms around, shouting at the animals and somehow managing to create a sort of break in the flow. Then, gradually, they all started to reverse and *baaaaaa* and edge out of the place, leaving a smell of wet wool behind, which isn't the most pleasant of smells if you aren't used to it. Sam broke out of the flock, his face bright red, his blue eyes shocked and his fair hair all messy. As those eyes caught mine, I felt my heart judder. Sam always had that effect on me.

Sam and I had a bit of a history, and I'd largely managed to avoid him for quite some time — until tonight, really . . . but we'll get to that later.

This was weird though. Very weird, because here he was, right in front of me, and we were doing that thing where you both stare at each other and you don't really know what to say or do. But I couldn't have let him get trampled by the sheep, no matter what had gone on. I just couldn't.

I think Sam had the advantage in the situation. He was in his own clothes for a start, and didn't have fake dirt smeared all over his face or dark shadows drawn under his eyes to imply he was a starving pauper. Even though I was only an extra, they'd still gone to town on the make-up.

My hair looked like a rats' nest under the bonnet, so it was probably a good job my dark tresses were hidden away.

'Cerys! Thank God. I don't know whether to be eternally grateful or immensely embarrassed that I had to be saved by you.'

''s the least I can do,' I mumbled, feeling my face flush. He *also* always had that effect on me. 'Anyway, I think Edie wants more wine, so I couldn't let you die, could I?' I shooed a couple of rogue animals out and soon there was just that sheepy smell left in the pub, amidst grumbling regulars checking their drinks for lanolin and bits of fleece. I wrinkled my nose and smiled, half-embarrassed that my talents lay in sheep-herding and not in seduction. 'Or let you get dyed in the wool. Ha ha.' Then I stared blankly at him and he stared blankly at me, because, like I'd just said, I'm rubbish at seduction and also not very good at making jokes. 'Ha ha,' I tried again. And, even to me, it sounded pathetic and not at all like the first thing I should have chosen to say to Lovely Sam, having just saved his life. 'Ha ha . . .' I felt the smile slip off my face. I really did not know when to shut up. I realised this wasn't going to be the best way to make him see the delightful, fun-filled person I knew I was, or, indeed, lead him to see sense and fall for me — hard. 'Ha . . .'

Anyway, I wasn't even sure why I was trying to give that impression. I was onto a loser regardless because, unfortunately, Lovely Sam was not just lovely, he was also one half of 'Belinda-and-Sam'. Or 'Blam! You know. Just like Wham!' as Edie had described them, making their hideous coupledom sound like some sort of sound effect from a comic book. It wasn't very comical really, especially as Belinda didn't really seem to like Padcock, where Sam had been born and brought up. Over the last couple of years, I'd also noticed that Belinda had been, quite blatantly, disappearing off to London as much as she could. But, despite all of this, and as much as I'd lost sleep over Sam and dreamed silly daydreams

11

about how super we'd be together, the fact remained that he was still half of Blam!

I tore my gaze away from him and studied a piece of tinsel that was hanging wonkily off the coat-stand. I think it had been disturbed by the rampaging sheep. I focused on that tinsel and tried *not* to focus on the events that had brought us here, to this very, very awkward point.

I'd managed to avoid him during most of the spring through into the summer, by going to a pub a couple of miles away on the canal side — Edie and I had done lots of cycling as a result, so the bonus was we worked off the calories we drank. Edie must have thought I was mad to suggest such extreme physical exercise when there was a perfectly good pub in our village, and the days that she genuinely did grumble and groan and claim she 'couldn't possibly', we *had* gone to the Spatchcock — but stayed in the beer garden, so I didn't have to actually go inside too much.

The only reason I was inside today was

the fact that we'd all gone in after that filming and, for some silly reason, I'd figured that as I was in disguise, I could just sit in the corner and he wouldn't notice me.

That was until the sheep had come in, and I'd automatically lurched over there like a big lumpen thing to save him.

The whole situation was utterly painful. Truth be told, I'd fallen in love with Lovely Sam in the first ten minutes of meeting him, and that had been an embarrassingly long time ago — we're not talking in terms of weeks here, or even months. We're talking *four years*.

2

Christmas Past

Four years ago

So here I was in Padcock — the place where I was about to start my new life. My boxes of possessions were in the flat above the shop, and I was downstairs ready to take the first step towards forgetting all about my ex-boyfriend, Rhys. I was standing outside, admiring my new shop front, imagining the signage and wondering if I needed some colourful blinds at the windows.

It had been quite clinical really, dividing all our stuff up, but I hadn't expected anything different. Back in North Wales, when all that had been going on, I'd stood in the empty music room of our fairly large stone-built house as the December sun poured in through the big window. The curtains were still hanging up. They were cream silk and pooled onto the brightly coloured carpet that matched the colour I'd painted the fireplace. I realised I felt more emotionally attached to those curtains than I did to Rhys, which probably demonstrated how little I cared for him at that point.

We hadn't put a Christmas tree up that year. No surprise there. Rhys had told me at the end of September that he was moving out, and he'd gone within a week or so — to his new girlfriend's house, I'd found out later. It somehow fell to me to get the place in North Wales sold as quickly as I could, and decorations were just one more thing to take down. The new owners wanted to be in by Christmas anyway.

After the break-up, I knew it was time for me to cut my losses and to follow a dream. Everything I had built up in Wales had sort of crumbled into Christmas cake crumbs, and I really, really needed a fresh start. So, I was finally going to open that craft shop I'd yearned to have, and I was going to run my little tea room and forget everything else. I was hopeful that I might even find it in me to start playing my guitar again. I hadn't had the headspace in those final days and weeks with Rhys. There was too much else to be thinking about.

But it was the beginning of December.

And it was only a few weeks until Christmas.

And I was in Padcock.

In fact, when I'd arrived in Padcock for the 'Christmas of New Beginnings', as I'd christened it, I hadn't thought for one moment that I might have made a mistake by ditching my old life and moving to the village.

Everything had been fine and dandy in Wales before Rhys and I split up, and, to be fair, it would have *continued* to be fine and dandy afterwards, had my brother and his girlfriend not split up before us.

It made it worse, in some ways, that Geraint's girlfriend, Alwen, had decided *she* wanted to make a new life with our cousin, Dylan. The four of us had been in a folk group together — not only was I a Border collie, you see, I was a musical

Border collie — and we'd started playing at some pubs and clubs and festivals, and made quite a name for ourselves. I played guitar and sang, my brother played the fiddle and sang, Alwen played the flute, and Dylan sang along with the backing and played a banjo.

But once Alwen and Dylan got together, that was the end of it. I couldn't stand Geraint's trembling bottom lip every time he encountered her, or the deep, heaving sighs every time he wanted to talk about her. We'd tried for a little while to go it alone as a duo, but he was way too emotional and ended up making me and the audience feel rubbish. He always wanted to play miserable songs and effectively brought the mood down wherever he went — which was another good reason not to be spending Christmas that year *en famille*. We always had a huge family 'do', which involved the aunts, uncles and, oh yes, the cousins. I'd decided I wanted to be well away from it all, because the parents and aunts and uncles had no sense of how awkward it would all end up being. To them, we were still children and Geraint's heart-break over Alwen simply an infatuation that could easily be brushed aside.

To Geraint, she was the love of his life, so the 'childish infatuation' thing was not going to hold water.

And the absolute idiot was determined to go to the family bash and win her back.

I did *not* want to be part of that. It's a bit uncomfortable, isn't it, witnessing your older brother acting like a teenager? Next thing we knew, he'd be drawing a heart with their initials in biro on his hand and kissing his pillow.

So, no.

No thank *you*.

This was the reason I'd chosen to spend Christmas in my new home in Padcock, away from my brother's doomed love life. And away from mine. Rhys still riled me whenever I thought about him and, to be honest, I didn't even want to be in the same country as him at that point.

I broke away from my thoughts and

let myself into my lovely new shop, deciding that the unpacking of boxes could wait a little while. I stared in awe and excitement at the blank walls in the space, wondering about the best way to display stuff, and then *he* popped his head through the open door and smiled that massive smile of his and said, 'Hey. I'm Sam Mackintosh. I own the pub. Is there anything you need?'

And that was it. I was smitten, as they say.

Yet my inspired response went something like: 'Ummm. Maybe a ladder? And a feather duster? Oh, and, by the way, I'm Cerys Davies, I'm from Wales and I just broke up with an idiot.' Then I pointed to the top corner of the shop where there was a literal tarantula swinging around in a massive cobweb.

Sam stepped inside and, to his credit, didn't comment on the 'I've broken up with an idiot' bit, because why should it have mattered to him, really? Then he looked up as well, standing close enough to me so I could smell his aftershave, which was — *and still is* — sort of orangey and spicy and piney, and made me think of Christmas again.

'Ahhh, he's just a little one.' He looked at me sideways and grinned. 'He's doing no harm, but I'll evict him for you if you want — he can explore somewhere else.'

I nodded dumbly — a *little* one? — and he reached up, cupped his hands and ever-so-gently retrieved the spider and released him outside.

'Padcock must breed huge spiders if he's just little.'

'Just wait until his dad comes looking for him.' Sam winked and I giggled girlishly and stupidly — I may even have twiddled my hair a bit (*cringe!*) — and then continued standing there like a dork, waiting for him to say something else. *Like what?* I hear you ask. *Oooh, I don't know, perhaps something like 'Gosh you're really pretty and I'd like to take you out sometime.'* But, of course, he didn't say that.

Instead, he said: 'Oh — is that your guitar?' He nodded at my trusty guitar which was propped up against the wall. I'd had rather a bizarre idea about playing it in the premises while the room was still empty so I could see what the acoustics were like. I'd reasoned that if I could play alone, nobody would be bothered by the noise, and I could lose myself in my music for a while, which was something I had always liked to do.

'Yes — ummmm — yes. Why, yes it *is*. It *is* my guitar. It *is* . . .' My voice petered out, and I stopped twisting fake ringlets into my straight dark hair.

'I'm always looking for live music to put on in the pub. So, if it's something you'd consider doing, I'd love to chat about it. Pop along and see me, once you're settled in, and we can sort something out.' He must have seen the look of horror that flickered across my face. I hadn't played in public for ages — and the thought of doing it in front of a crowd right now terrified me. 'Or not,' he added, smiling reassuringly. 'Hey, I'm sorry. No pressure! I just got excited. The Spatchcock absolutely needs something to put it on the map.' This time, I saw his eyes flicker a little uncertainly, but then the expression was gone and his smile was as warm as ever. I couldn't stop staring at him. 'A USP — a unique selling point. Or so I've been told. Anyway. Doesn't matter. It was lovely to meet you.'

'Thanks. It was . . . lovely . . . to meet you too. Thanks for, you know, rescuing me from the tarantula.'

'You're very welcome. But please — if you do decide you'd be able to play, give me a call, okay?' Our eyes locked and I saw that his were a startling shade of bright blue.

'*Urrmphhgggsstttt . . .*' I said. My default setting was 'burbling idiot' when I couldn't think of the right thing to say, and my default setting today also involved not being able to tear my gaze away from his. '*Blhhsgfff . . .*' I finished pathetically, shaking my head.

Sam grinned. 'Okay, that's fine. Please. Don't worry about — it was just an idea. If you change your mind, you know where I am . . . but, actually, no you don't, do you? Come here, I'll show you.' He turned and I followed him, and we stood close together in the doorway, me peering around his body as he pointed right. 'That's the pub there, just along the road. See it? Actually, it's the only pub in the village so, yeah.' It was his turn to look at me and shake his head. 'Stupid. You'll know which one it is, as there aren't any more. Okay — I'm off, before you think we're all crazy in Padcock. Bye, Cerys. It was good to meet you. I'll see you around, I'm sure.' And he stepped out of the shop and headed in the direction of his pub.

I was left staring after him, completely speechless, and looking particularly dork-like as he strode off down the street — and right into the arms of a gorgeous brunette.

I pulled myself together instantly, trying to work out, rather hopelessly, if she could be his sister — *or even just a good friend or neighbour, perhaps?* — when a small, curvaceous blonde appeared, trailing along the road and blowing her nose into a soggy tissue before drawing to a halt outside my shop. She looked as if she'd been crying, still was to some extent, and we stared at each other with one of those instant senses of kindred-spirit connection — although we were, quite literally, complete opposites to look at. The blonde had wisps of chin-length hair coming loose from a scraggy little paintbrush-sized ponytail and inch-long dark roots. My hair was almost jet-black and hung straight down to the middle of my back, bluntly cut with a thick fringe. The girl was wearing a tartan mini skirt and a black polo neck jumper, thick black woolly tights and knee-length black boots. Her blacker-than-black eye make-up was smudged and she was sniffing miserably.

'Are you all right?' I asked instinctively.

'Not really. My gran died and this is the first Christmas I've spent without her. I've just been to the churchyard to see her. It's not the same. Not really. I'm

Edie, by the way.'

'Hello, Edie. I'm Cerys. I've just moved in.'

Edie nodded. 'I know. You're the talk of the village. I see you've already met Sam.' She indicated the man who was now some way in the distance. 'He's lovely. His girlfriend is awful. She's called Belinda.' She pulled a face. 'I don't like her. But Sam is lovely. He's very lovely.' Her bottom lip trembled, and I reached out to touch her arm. I'm one of these people who cries along with other people — unless it's Geraint, of course — so my bottom lip had started to tremble too. 'Come in,' I said. 'I was just about to put the kettle on. If it makes it any better, I can tell you how rubbish my ex was and we can call him names?'

'Okay.' Edie nodded, wiped her nose on her sleeve and followed me inside. 'And I can tell you about a man I know who's doing something arty in London and is very undeserving of the attention. Ooh, cool guitar! I love Bob Dylan . . . although 'Forever Young' and

'Knockin' on Heaven's Door' make me very sad. But I still love him. Who d'you love, Cerys?'

'Ooh. I love Bob Dylan too. But I tell you who I don't love. And that's my ex. He hates Bob Dylan. And he hates folk music in general. And d'you know, that's what I do — or did. Rhys said I was rubbish and the group I was in was ridiculous, and who did we think we were, the 'Bloody Corrs'? And that's exactly what he said. The 'Bloody Corrs'.'

'But they're Irish.' Edie looked at me in confusion. 'They're an Irish band. And you don't sound Irish.'

'That's because I'm not.' I ushered her through the little door to my flat and we headed upstairs, where we were immediately surrounded by all the things I had yet to unpack. But the kettle was working, and I had tea, coffee, milk, mugs and biscuits, so I knew we'd be fine. 'I'm Welsh. As is my brother, my cousin and the other person in the band. I told him that as well — that I wasn't Irish and he should know that. And we weren't the

'Bloody Corrs'. Then he said, fine, you're not exactly Katherine Jenkins either, are you? And then he said my playing annoyed him, and my singing put his teeth on edge, and nobody in their right minds should be paying good money to listen to a second-rate 'Bloody Corrs' band and we needed a reality check.'

'Oh my, that's dreadful!' Edie was aghast, and it felt good ranting about it to her. I couldn't stop myself from continuing.

'*And* there was a load of hassle between our band members at that time, and all I wanted was a sounding board and a bit of support from him, and *then* he laughed and said we'd never be Fleetwood Mac either, so it was just as well the band seemed to breaking up as it would give me more time to do something that paid more money.' I shrugged and felt my bottom lip wobble a bit. I rubbed my eyes with the back of my hand and then rubbed my nose. The tears weren't very far away, and I wondered whether I'd ever get my confidence back with my music. But it felt better saying all that out loud. Better — but also very raw. Rhys had really, really upset me that day, and it wasn't the first time he'd been disparaging. Although I realised that particular incident *had* been the time when I'd actually started to believe him.

Which is why, once the band had gasped out its last, I'd had no interest in performing again.

Perhaps I really was rubbish.

'Your ex,' Edie announced, 'is an arse. Let me make you a cuppa — just show me where everything is.'

And from that moment, she was my best friend.

★ ★ ★

Edie and I ended up spending Christmas Day together — my very first Padcock Christmas — at her gran's cottage, where she was currently living. My flat was still in no fit state to entertain really.

Our intention was to eat fuss-free microwave turkey ready meals, consume our own combined bodyweight in chocolate and drink far too much wine, wrapping it all up in a super-fun day.

'I've made a tick-list,' she informed me, flinging the door open to me at 9 a.m. when I rocked up ready for the day in my snowflake-patterned leggings, my festive jumper which said *Naughty and Nice* in sequins, and my slippers that were shaped like green and red elfin boots, complete with proper jingle-bells on the toes. She waved a funky psychedelic-coloured sheet she had clearly torn out of a notebook at me. It was entitled *Jolly List* and had four big, blocky lines of writing on, which went something like this:

Consume Cerys and Edie's combined bodyweight in chocolate
Drink far too much nice fizzy wine
Eat fuss-free microwave turkey ready meals
Have a super-fun day, yay!!!!!!!

'Easy,' I said. 'Nothing can go wrong!' But we kind of fell down at Point

Three, because, after doing quite well on Points One and Two, once we had taken the ready meals out of Edie's fridge and opened their cartons and read the actually quite detailed instructions, we realised they weren't simple, fuss-free microwave meals at all. In fact, it seemed that we would have to put lots of the Christmas lunch elements in at different times, and therefore keep an eye on it all, and therefore miss parts of Edie's favourite Christmas TV film, *Holiday Inn*, which she insisted on calling 'White Christmas' because of the Bing Crosby song in it. Delaying lunch, she informed me, was not an option, because then it impacted on her other favourite Christmas TV film: *Willy Wonka and the Chocolate Factory*.

'This,' she muttered quite darkly, whilst shaking the carton and simultaneously trying to establish at what time the pigs-in-blankets would have to go in the oven, 'impacts quite severely on Point Four. And I feel very, very stupid and very, very sorry that I bought these things from Sally's corner shop. I may have ruined Christmas. What shall we do, Cerys? What shall we *do*?'

But before we could decide what to do — we'd been discussing substituting Point Three for a big bowl of Frosties and milk, or just going straight to pudding — there was a knock at her door.

We looked at each other in horror. *Who on earth could be knocking on Edie's door at lunchtime on Christmas Day?*

'Who on earth could be knocking on my door at lunchtime on Christmas Day?' Edie asked, almost in a whisper. 'I'm not expecting anyone.'

'Me neither,' I replied. Which was rather a stupid thing to say, because it was obviously Edie's house and not mine, so why would anyone try to seek me out here, at lunchtime, on Christmas Day? But we were, bear in mind, doing extraordinarily well on Point Two at this point. 'I'll go and check,' I said when I noticed Edie standing there staring at the door like she didn't really know what to do, tears beginning to well up in her eyes. It *was* her first Christmas on her own without her gran, and it was clear that she'd wanted the day to be structured — well, structured in as much of an 'Edie' sort of way as it could be, hence her 'Jolly List'. I'd realised she was very fragile and this odd interruption wasn't in her game plan, so she didn't really know how to cope with it.

Edie just nodded, and I shuffled along the small hallway in my jingly slippers, straightened my pink fluffy angel halo headband — one of Edie's gifts to me — and opened the door.

'Merry Christmas.' Sam was standing there, his smile brightening up the disappointingly drizzly day. I noticed he was also wearing a festive jumper — it had a reindeer on it with flashing lights, *genuine* flashing lights, wound around its antlers and a happy, drunken expression on its face as it stood next to what had been, I guessed, a large glass of sherry it'd stolen from Santa.

'Merry Christmas,' I responded, my cheeks heating up and my knees buckling just a little. I now realised that I hadn't been exaggerating Sam's gorgeousness in my head at all — he *was* gorgeous, and I hadn't been able to stop thinking of him since I'd first met him a couple of weeks ago. 'I'm so sorry I haven't been to the pub. I've been so busy getting organised . . . also I'm sorry I haven't talked to you about live music and stuff.'

It was a stupid thing to say to him, it really was, but part of me, still scarred by Rhys' rude and arrogant behaviour, thought that Sam had come to the door to tell me off for not pursuing the live music thing.

'What? Oh! Oh no. That's fine. It was just something to think about. Look — can these go to a good home, do you think?'

I realised then that Sam was holding two large cardboard container things up. As he lifted them towards me, my nose twitched and I could smell the unmistakeable aroma of a freshly-cooked Christmas lunch.

'Are they turkey dinners? *Real* turkey

dinners?' I looked at him and he nodded.

'They are. I begged our chef to plate
two up for you. Sally's husband is in
the pub and we got chatting, and he
said that Edie had been in buying some
ready meals and was all excited about
a fuss-free dinner for the pair of you. I
have experience of these dinners.' He
shook his head slowly and dramatically.
'And they are *not* fuss-free. I bought
one myself a couple of years ago and,
seriously, who can be bothered to time
pigs-in-blankets to the exact minute and
work out when the roasties go in, and
then spend ages scraping burnt gravy
out of the container because you messed
up your timings? Not me.'

'Nor us.' I cast a glance back into the
kitchen. 'Edie's tried to do her best, but
she's feeling bad about it, and I don't
want her to miss her 'White Christmas'
film or *Willy Wonka*, and I was just about
to pour the Frosties into the bowls,
so . . .' I looked down at the boxes, now
feeling the warmth rising from them on

my face. 'This means so much to us. To her. Thank you. Thank you so much for thinking about us.'

Sam handed the boxes over to me and our fingers connected for the briefest second, causing my skin to tingle. I told myself it was just the heat from the boxes, but I knew that was only me fooling myself.

'Enjoy them. Do you want pudding? I can send someone over with some of that too.'

'Oh, pudding is sorted,' I said, smiling up at him. 'We're going to work on Point One of our list, and we've got a microwave chocolate sponge ready. One of those where you get the chocolatey custard with it. And we'll have it with brandy cream. Delicious.'

'Point One?' To give him his due, he simply laughed and shook his head mock-despairingly. 'I'm not even going to ask. But, hey, have an amazing day, okay? And Merry Christmas again.'

'Thank you. Again. Oh! But how much do I owe you?'

'Nothing.' He put his hands in his pockets. 'From me to you, as a gift.'

'Are you sure?'

'Yes. I'm sure. Maybe one day, I'll get you to be my live music person. We can call it quits then, eh?' Then he winked and turned away, and I stared after him until he rounded the corner and I couldn't see him any more.

'Lunch is served,' I said, as I came back into the kitchen. 'Courtesy of Sam. He really *is* lovely, isn't he?'

Edie's eyes lit up, and she immediately pounced on the boxes and ripped one open. 'Oh my! Oh, I'll have to thank him properly when I next see him. And yes — yes, he *is* lovely. Lovely Sam.'

'Lovely Sam,' I echoed, opening the other box and sniffing appreciatively. 'Lovely Sam indeed.'

And by the end of the day, our Jolly List looked something like this:

Consume Cerys and Edie's combined body-weight in chocolate — tick
Drink far too much nice fizzy wine —

double-tick
Eat fuss-free microwave turkey ready meals — NO! BUT WE LOVE LOVELY SAM!!!!
Have a super-fun day, yay!!!!!!! — tick, tick, tick!

And thus, upon my first Christmas Day in Padcock, it came to pass that Lovely Sam was christened 'Lovely Sam', and I decided I was properly, irrefutably and totally in love with him.

And I kept the Jolly List. Just because I could.

3

Christmas Past

Three years ago

Belinda didn't like me.

I knew she didn't like me, and that was okay, because I didn't like her either. She always looked down her perfect nose at me, and whenever she came into the craft shop, she'd only ever poke around and turn that very same nose up at the things I had in.

And she didn't eat cake either, which I found unreal.

But, despite Awful Belinda (yes, that was a name that had also stuck) and the fact that she sometimes made me feel that my lovely little shop was a dingy little hole, I was determined that my second Christmas in Padcock would be something special. I also decided that Awful Belinda wouldn't take my Christmas spirit away, and that I would make the craft shop and tea room super festive; yes, I *fully* intended to go over the top with decorations and tinsel. I was very satisfied when I finished and took a step back to admire my work — the place looked so cheerful. I'd also had a little log-burner installed, and we'd decorated that too, so it all looked beautifully cosy and everyone exclaimed how delightful it was when they walked in.

Well, everyone except Belinda — but *that* wasn't surprising.

Edie certainly had an eye for making the place festive *and* funky, and, with her help, it really did look fabulous. The previous Christmas I'd hardly done anything except move in — and have a super-fun Christmas Day with Edie, of course. But by now, Edie was working with (for) me and we had quite a little success story going on. We'd created a place where friends would gather to gossip over cake, people would come to quietly read with a coffee, and the school mums would converge on after dropping their little darlings off. Although Belinda didn't have any children, she would often hold court there with a couple of her yummy mummy friends, and had also taken to sometimes turning up alone with a lap-top — but, as I said, she would *not* eat cake.

Apart from today. Today, she ordered a small piece of vegan carrot cake very loudly.

'Just a small piece of the VEGAN CARROT CAKE.' Then she wrinkled her nose, peered at my cakes and spoke in her normal voice. 'The cakes *are* organic, aren't they?'

'Yes, Belinda.'

And even as I said that, a little voice in my head went: *As organic as the milk you don't have in your coffee. As organic as the locally sourced bacon, sausages and eggs you don't have in your breakfast butties. And I know you aren't a vegan, because Sam told me when he bought you some lemon and sea-salt chocolate, which I bet you didn't eat, so really the fact you asked specifically and loudly for 'vegan carrot cake' instead of 'carrot cake', like everyone else would, is clearly only for effect.* Fortunately, the little voice stayed in my head and my real voice said, more pleasantly than I *felt* like saying: 'The cakes are as organic as everything else in here. The clue is somewhat in the name of the establishment. Eclectically Yours — Cerys' Craft Shop and Organic Tea Room.' I smiled at her, although I didn't really mean it to be friendly. The fact was I ran a business, and so long as my hands were clenched under the counter-top so she couldn't see me digging my nails into my palms in anger, I could afford to at least pretend to be polite.

'We've got some nice turkey and cranberry quiche in,' said Edie, lolling against the counter with a pen stuck into her stubby ponytail. I think the word I'd have used to describe her in that moment would have been 'insouciant'. 'You might enjoy that. Very festive.'

'I don't think so.' Belinda shook her head and wandered over to her usual table where her friends were already waiting for her. 'Oh!' She sat down and looked over at us then clicked her fingers as if she was in the Ritz or something. We both stared at her. She clicked them again and we stared a little longer. Then she flushed and shouted, 'No cream on the cake.'

Again, we stared at her until she flushed an even brighter shade of red and turned away.

'I don't think you offered her cream, did you?' asked Edie.

I shook my head slowly. 'Nope.'

'Hmmm. Just making a point then,' she muttered.

'Appears so.' I shook my head in despair and busied myself cutting a wee-ny-sized slice of cake. Really — was it even worth it?

'Anyway, forget about her,' said Edie. 'Where do you think we should get a tree from?'

'A Christmas tree?' I looked around the premises. We only had about five tables and the rest of the place was taken up by the craft shop and the log-burner. 'I'm not actually sure that we've got room for one.'

We already had fairy lights up and jolly wooden snowmen and Santas everywhere. Edie had done some lovely pictures of the village in winter, and we had packs of Christmas cards and postcards made up from her designs dotted around, and the accompanying prints hung on the walls. There were festive nibbles, and jams and preserves and chocolates on the shelves, along with beautiful handmade ornaments, artisan soaps, bath salts and gifts aplenty — I couldn't see how I'd be able to cram in much more. I was planning to have a sherry and mince pie evening with Christmas music playing, and hopefully sell quite a few bits and bobs then — but I'd never really considered a tree.

'Not inside perhaps, but we could get one for outside. Sam does it at the pub. He has two, and they look really sweet — in little tubs by the front door. Of course, he always puts a big one up inside as well, but I don't think we'll manage that here, to be fair. Then you keep the little tree in the pot and each year it grows and grows . . .' Edie made 'getting bigger' motions with her arms. At least I think that's what she was doing. They were either 'getting bigger' motions or she was flailing her arms around pretending to be a windmill. 'It's kind of a tradition. The person who owns the pub has always done it. Even when I was a child, there'd always be a tree outside.'

'Sounds gorgeous.' I smiled at her. 'Okay — the cake is ready, there's no cream in sight. Don't you think she looks a bit excitable today?' I nodded across to Belinda, and she did indeed have a gleam in her eye.

'So, girlies, I have the *best* news. I'm so excited!' Her voice rang out around the shop and my stomach lurched. For one hideous moment, I thought she might be about to announce that she was engaged. I didn't quite know how I would feel about that.

I was struggling to see why Sam stuck with her really, never mind thinking about him marrying her. I almost didn't want to hear what she had to say next.

'I'm starting my own fashion business!' she squealed. 'Accessories, jewellery, scarves. Then when I'm established, I'll branch out. Knitwear is always a good one — bobble hats, gloves. Those super cute, thick knitted headbands that you wear on a cosy wintry walk.' She indicated a circle around her head, and I knew she meant those silly things that leave the crown of your head freezing and muffle your ears. Everyone knows that heat rises, and therefore heat leaves the top of your head first, so that was the most important part to cover, surely! However, by the way her acolytes hooted and screeched back — 'Oh darling, *such* a good idea!' and, 'Yes! Cashmere. Of *course*!' — I figured I was going to be tarred as the poor provincial girl who didn't understand the desirability of circular non-head warmers if I dared express an opinion on the matter.

'What is the point of a woolly dough-nut that doesn't keep your head warm?' hissed Edie in my ear, and I couldn't help but nod. I was pleased she agreed with me.

'I'm glad you're provincial too, Edie. Even though you're from Camden.'

'Eh?'

But I shook my head and picked up the tray. 'I'll take it over.'

As expected, they all ignored me as I set the drinks and snacks down on the table, but I was still listening to Belinda go on with her grandiose plans. 'Of course, it means I'll have to spend some time in the City,' she said thoughtfully. 'I can't think of a better excuse to get away from this awful little place anyway,' she half muttered under her breath.

'Where will you stay? Will you rent somewhere?' asked one of her friends.

'God, no. I've still got the mews house. I'll use that.'

That did make me stop in my tracks. Belinda had a mews house in London?

'I thought you might have sold it by now.'

'Gosh, no.' Here, she leaned forward and smirked. 'A girl has to have an escape plan.'

I may have smacked down a plate of cake a little too hard at that point because Belinda looked up at me, startled.

Ha, I thought. *Yes, you can say stuff like that all you like, but remember I can hear you and nothing is a secret in here.*

'Of course,' she tittered, quite fakely, 'I'm joking. I love it here and wouldn't want to be away from my gorgeous boyfriend any longer than absolutely necessary.'

It may have been my imagination, but I was pretty sure she'd added emphasis on the words 'my gorgeous boyfriend'. Was she warning me off? If so, I had no idea why. It was true that I'd loved Sam for ages, but not once had I ever thought he liked me back in any way other than as a friend — which was the way it should be, let's be honest.

The man was in a long-term relationship, after all.

And even if I didn't agree with his choice of girlfriend, who was I to change his opinion anyway? Edie persuaded me

47

to go and get the Christmas tree the very next morning. 'I'll look after the shop,' she said as soon as she burst in. 'You go and choose a tree. Now.'

'What? From where?'

'Ummm — the Christmas Tree Farm?' She looked at me oddly, as if I should have known. She'd forgotten, I guess, that I was still a relative newbie in Padcock. It was only my second Christmas here, after all.

'Where?'

'It's a farm. Down that way.' She gestured wildly with one of her flailing windmill arm movements down the road. 'They do Christmas trees. You go and pick one, and they sell it to you. Simple.'

'Oh. Right.' I remained standing in the middle of the shop, bemused for a moment. I knew I needed a tree, but to be told to go and get one right at that very moment had thrown me a bit.

'Shoo.' Edie pushed me out of the door and, for good measure, pointed back down the street. 'That way. Straight down the road, five miles or so, then you'll see the sign. Get a nice one!' And with that, I found myself in the street, looking, I suspect, pretty confused.

'You look confused.'

I jumped and turned at the voice.

'Sam! Gosh. Hello! You've just confirmed my suspicions. I *am* confused. I am *very* confused,' I responded, flushing hotly.

He grinned. I knew, in that moment, where I'd seen a grin of that beauty before — Marti Pellow from the pop group Wet Wet Wet. I was only a child in the nineties, but some things just make an impression on you, don't they?

Marti's grin was one of them, and Sam's grin was exactly like it. I felt like Love was indeed All Around Us, well, All Around *Me* in the shape of Love(ly) Sam, anyway.

'And why are you confused?' He folded his arms and leaned back against the wall. 'Is it because you're unsure how to approach me to ask about a slot in my live music programme?' Then he pushed himself away from the wall and leaned in towards me, whispering in my ear, 'Not that I *have* a live music programme. I just think if there are any local industry spies around, they need to assume I *do* have a USP.'

The scent of that spicy, orangey aftershave tickled my nose, and I couldn't help closing my eyes and taking a surreptitious sniff.

I found myself whispering back, 'I'm not unsure how to approach you about the live music programme, because me being involved ain't ever going to happen.' Then I stood up and, reluctantly, made some distance between us. I glanced at him and he was looking at me curiously, an amused little half-smile on his lips which told me this was a discussion that was going to be ongoing throughout my time in Padcock. 'And I actually look confused because Edie says I should go to a Christmas Tree Farm down that way—' I jabbed my forefinger down the road, exactly as Edie had done '—and choose a tree for outside the tea room.

That's it!' I shrugged helplessly. 'Yes, her instructions were *that* vague. Hence why I look confused.'

'Ah.' Sam nodded thoughtfully. 'I can see how that might be confusing. But it's lucky I bumped into you.' He unfolded his arms and jangled some car keys at me. 'I'm heading there now myself. In fact, I'd just told Edie that when I met her in the street about five minutes ago. I wondered why she'd run off.'

'The girl loves her Christmas trees. She did say I needed to get one, and she did say you put two outside the pub every year, and one inside. Two birds with one stone.'

'Indeed. The two outdoor ones are in pots, currently hidden in the beer garden, so that's fine, but I do need to get a cut one for the bar. Why don't you come with me? It'll save you trying to find the place on your own, and I've got the van so it'll be easier for you to transport. No catches. I won't try to talk you into playing at the Spatchcock while we travel. Promise.'

'Oh! Oh yes. That sounds great. The trip, I mean. Not playing at the Spatchcock, of course. But yes. A great idea! The trip is a great idea!' I smiled back at him, surprising myself with the enthusiasm to which I'd agreed to a trip in a van to a muddy old farm.

It was only as I was strapping myself into the passenger seat that I wondered, for one very brief moment, whether Edie had thrown us together a little deliberately.

Then I also remembered that she'd been encouraging me to be 'more musical, Cerys, you do play and sing very well, and Rhys is *definitely* an arse,' after she'd wandered in too early one morning and caught me on the hop, playing my guitar and singing one of my favourite folk songs when I thought nobody would hear me. *Were the pair of them in cahoots?*

I didn't know how I should feel about that.

I didn't have too long to ponder it, mind you. It didn't take us an enormous amount of time to get to the Christmas Tree Farm. It was quite exciting, actually, as we pulled up into the car park. The smell of pine hit my nose almost as soon as I set foot outside, and there were already a few groups of enthusiastic people in front of us choosing their trees.

A man with rosy cheeks and a big smile was standing by a giant netting machine, and I knew he'd be feeding the trees through it once people had made their selections so that they'd all come out kind of shrink-wrapped and ready to be taken home; the trees, that is — not the people.

Sam and I wandered around the displays, the fairy lights strung between the branches of the big trees still in the ground (lucky them) looking super pretty. There'd been a hard frost overnight, and the sight of the twinkly white branches and the silver-coated trunks of the Christmas trees made me feel quite jolly.

Small trees, potted in red and green buckets, were standing in lines next to their bigger neighbours, and I pounced on one of the smallest. 'This one will do me,' I said, picking it up. 'Not too big to keep putting inside the shop every night.'

'Why would you want to put it away every night?' Sam looked down at me curiously.

'Well, in case anyone steals it.'

'Nobody in Padcock is low enough to be a Christmas Tree Thief.'

'I don't know that though, do I?'

'No, but I do.' He grinned again and I clutched the tree more tightly, hoping if I concentrated on hanging onto that, my knees might not feel quite so weak at the sight of that smile. 'You could get a bigger one. What about this one?' He stopped suddenly and leaned down in front of me. I closed my eyes, not knowing whether to be thankful that I hadn't actually walked into him, fallen over and landed flat on my face right next to him, or disappointed that I'd managed to stop that from happening.

Because if I *had* done that, he'd have no doubt held out his hand to me and helped me up.

It was almost worth taking a step and doing it . . . just to see.

But no. I didn't.

Of course, I didn't.

Instead, I found myself mentioning Belinda.

Ugh.

'No — I've picked up this one now.' I lifted the tiny tree up to show him. 'It's a living thing. It'll feel rejected if I put it back. Oh . . . and I meant to say . . . I overheard Belinda saying she's starting a new business up. That's good, isn't it?' Even to me, my voice sounded falsely bright.

Sam straightened up and, momentarily, a look of something strangely regretful flickered across his face. He shrugged. 'Yes, it is ... I suppose. She's always wanted to do something like that. She's following her dream, so that's great for her.' He reached out and fiddled with a stray pinecone on one of the bigger trees.

'But not so great for you?' The words

were out before I could stop them, and he looked at me quickly. 'Sorry. None of my business. I shouldn't have mentioned it.'

'No, it's okay.' He smiled again, a little ruefully this time though. 'It's just she's already told me she'll be spending most of the week in London — that came as a bit of a shock, to be honest. She was . . .' He shrugged again. 'Well, she was renting the mews house out — it's her house, to be fair, but with her living here it didn't make any sense to have it standing there empty, really — and the first I knew of this London idea was when she told me she'd given the tenants notice and wanted them out by Christmas.'

How Scrooge-y! I wanted to shout. I was horrified. I truly thought only Victorian misers kicked people out in December.

'That's not very . . . nice,' I said instead, quite carefully.

'Hmmm. No. No, it's not nice at all. Also, the rental money is what she's using as capital for the new business. All in her 'life-plan', apparently. Never mind.' His smile switched on again. 'I'm sure she'll make a success of it. Good luck to her.'

'Oh.' I was silent for a moment, processing that. And then it slipped out, as it often does with me. 'The plan — her 'life-plan'. Had she never discussed it with you? What she wanted to do — in the future, kind of thing?'

He looked at me, and this time his smile was sad. 'You know, Cerys, I don't think she ever did. She doesn't like to look too far ahead — prefers to be spontaneous and sometimes she throws a curveball at me like that. She's a free spirit and she just laughs it off when I suggest maybe getting married or having kids. Still — we've only been together a couple of years, so there's plenty of time for all of that, isn't there?'

'Oh. Yes. I suppose so.' I didn't know what to say after that, so I hugged my tree tighter and said nothing at all.

'Anyway, are you sorted for Christmas lunch this year?' Sam asked. It seemed as if he was deliberately changing the subject.

'Ah. Yes. Edie and I are going to my brother's actually, in London. She's going to show me her flat in Camden Town and we're going to stay there for a couple of nights. Geraint only has a one-bedroom place, so it makes more sense for us to go to Edie's. I'm looking forward to it. Geraint is trying to avoid the family Christmas this year, after he showed himself up last year trying to win his ex back from our cousin — so he's making the excuse that he's working and says he'll go to Mum and Dad's after Boxing Day. I've told the parents I'll wait and go with him, and Edie will come back here on her own. Or she can wait until I come back to London, and we can travel down to Padcock together . . . Sorry, you don't need to hear all that.' I was appalled at myself for talking so much. 'You asked a very simple question and you got a ramble in response.'

'Oh, but I do need to hear it. I love your accent. I love to hear you talk. Don't apologise.' Sam grinned. 'So, if you're going to be in London, you won't need me to do a mercy dash with lunch this year, will you?'

'No. But I loved the fact you mercy dashed. It really was one of the best Christmas lunches I've ever had.'

'Thank you. I would, you know? I'd bring you one again if you wanted it. If you were in Padcock.'

I looked at him for a moment longer than I really should have done. 'It would be entirely worth it, to have Christmas here, and to have you turn up on my doorstep.' I gave myself a mental shake. 'With my lunch. Of course.'

'Of course. It would be worth it for me too, you know?'

'Really?'

'Really. Because then that's *two* live performances you'd owe me.'

Lovely Sam.

Of course it was.

Of course that was the reason — the only reason.

I hugged my tree even closer.

Of course.

4

Christmas Past

Two Years Ago

So, this year Edie had decided it would be a 'Good Thing' if we held a Christmas Craft Fair outside the tea room. 'All the little villages are doing it,' she said, munching her way thoughtfully through a toasted teacake in early December. We got fresh deliveries each day from the bakery down the road, and, if it was one of Edie's days in, she inevitably pounced on the roundest, most fruitiest-filled teacake and claimed it as her own.

'That sounds nice — but also labour intensive.' I set the dishwasher off, clearing up after the school mums had popped in for their morning cuppa, and then I set about making us each a coffee, enjoying the lull before the lunchtime rush.

There were a few people in the craft shop area browsing the shelves, and I noted that they were looking closely at the twiggy tree in the corner that Edie had draped with fairy lights and hung wooden, hand-carved decorations on. It wasn't really traditional, in the, well, *traditional* sense, but it looked beautiful and contemporary; especially the way she'd draped the stand with white muslin, dotted with tiny silver stars. Plus, it was all we had room for inside — space was at a premium, don't forget.

Edie leaned over and casually turned up our Christmas CD. It was playing 'Troika', my absolute favourite classical Christmas piece, and it instantly transported me to a world where I was riding in a sleigh, pulled through the snowy landscape by horses decked with silver bells. Of course, in this fantasy I was wearing a gorgeous nineteenth-century 'floofy dress', as Edie called them, and my handsome beau cracking the whip was . . . well. No contest. Nineteenth-century Sam was just as gorgeous as twenty-first-century Sam.

But then, in my daydream, Belinda

emerged in a scarlet crinoline from behind a snowman and started yelling at us, and I stopped imagining after that.

She spoiled everything, that woman.

'You pick your times to ask these things, don't you?' I cast a glance at a far too innocent-looking Edie. She knew 'Troika' made me melt.

'Come on. You know it makes sense. Let's do some market research.' She put down her plate, wiped her hands together to rid them of butter and crumbs, and then hollered, 'Hey! Excuse me, lovely customers!' The customers all turned and looked at her, slightly startled. But then she smiled one of those professional smiles she could come up with occasionally — she had attended and presented stuff at many, many important events in her previous life, after all — and they all smiled back.

'We're just wondering whether it would be a good idea if we did a Christmas Craft Fair in the street. Would you come, do you think? If we had, say, mulled wine and nibbles on as well? We could get the local craftspeople out and you could browse even more of their stock.'

'Oh!' One of the ladies nodded enthusiastically. 'That would be lovely. We often come to Padcock for a walk and a look around, and it would be a nice trip out.'

'Splendid,' said Edie and smiled again.

The other customers all nodded and verbalised their agreement. 'We've been to the summer fair at Padcock Court, but we've often said a Christmas one would be nice. With the streets and the shops and things all decorated. How pretty it would be,' another lady chipped in. Padcock Court was inhabited by a lady we had christened Mrs Pom-pom, due to the fact she wore pom-pom hats all year round. Her real name was Mrs Pomeroy, and she was a familiar sight around the village with her two hounds trailing behind her. The hounds were really two very elderly Labradors, Umbert and Arfur, who, when they barked, literally went 'Umf' and 'Arf'.

'A pretty Christmas Craft Fair. That's exactly what *we* thought,' replied Edie. 'Thank you. Watch out for the flyers then, we'll be sorting that out Very Soon.'

I could hear the capital letters in her confident declarations.

The customers all looked very cheerful and kept saying how nice it would be, even as we rang their craft shop purchases through the till.

When they'd left, I looked at Edie sternly. 'Now they're probably going to be waiting until the fair to buy anything else. We may have lost some sales there.'

'I don't think we did. In fact, I think we made more.' She shrugged, unconcerned, and I couldn't really argue with her.

But now we had a Christmas Craft Fair to organise.

And approximately three weeks to do it. But Edie was confident it would, 'all be fine, all be very fine indeed!'

And surprisingly, once the word went out, it didn't take too long to come together. All the horrible official stuff seemed to go through super-quickly; I was never quite sure who had pulled strings or where, but I was extremely grateful regardless. People like Belinda might have disliked living in Padcock, but I personally loved the community spirit in this place. All I'd had to do was mention the new fair and people flocked to help.

In fact, I was soon slightly concerned it was getting a little out of hand. And it was as I was holding a long list of people who'd requested tables and mentally working out where we could actually put them all, either by dotting them along the street, or spreading them out *across* the street, that Sam found me.

'Cerys! Great job.' He peered over my shoulder at the list, and my stomach somersaulted as the scent of his after-shave tickled my nose and his warm breath tickled my skin. It was a double-whammy.

'Sam. Hello.' I stepped back and turned to face him, mostly to put a bit of extra distance between us. 'I have to fit fifteen tables in. I think I need to spread it out. Do you think it'll cause traffic chaos if we close the street?'

'No, I don't suppose it will. The regulars know the shortcuts around the back of the cottages, and we can always put diversion signs up for anyone else. Any visitors can just park up at the pub, or in the grounds of Padcock Court.'

I felt the blood drain from my face. 'I didn't honestly think about visitors from outside the village — but of course. The ladies in the shop . . .' I shook my head, remembering the customers who had said they enjoyed visiting.

'It's not a problem. We just let them park where people park in the summer to visit the fair at the Court. Simple.' He shrugged his shoulders. 'I'll get in touch with the people who need to know about us closing the roads and we're good to go. Don't you worry about that.' He put his hand on my shoulder and squeezed it. I knew he meant the touch chummily and supportively, but I had to fight the urge to let my eyelids flutter and my knees buckle in a rather Victorian-style swoon. *Maybe I should invest in a 'floofy dress' after all . . .*

'Thanks, Sam. That would be appreciated. I'm maxed out with tables and was struggling to see what we could do. I didn't want people just walking past them all in a linear fashion. I wanted the visitors to mingle and see it all. Oh! Maybe I should see about using the village green instead.'

'No, it's notoriously boggy in the winter. The pond tends to seep under the grass, and you'd end up with buggies and prams and wheelchairs stuck, and wet children falling about and crying. Also crying parents, as they try to extract their little darlings from said mud, with audible *plops* and much snot.'

I couldn't help but laugh. He'd said it so seriously, and I could see the images so clearly, I found it terribly amusing. 'I loved mud when I was a child,' I said. 'It was especially good for pushing my brother into.'

'Wow — I never had you down as a

bully.' Sam grinned to show he was teasing.

'It was self-defence. I swear.'

'Sure, sure. Anyway, I'm glad I caught you. When do you want me to bring the moonshine down?'

'Moonshine?' I looked at him in confusion.

'Yes. Look.' He leaned over me again and pointed at my list. 'Table number seven. Local gin and fruit wines. That's me. I spoke to Edie about it.'

'You?' I looked at him in awe. 'You make it? And why didn't Edie tell me you'd booked a stall?'

'I do. And I don't know. Sorry.'

'Oh, well, that's very awesome that you make gin and fruit wine. Well, look — how about we put you next to me and my festive bakes? People might like a nice wine or some gin to take home with their gingerbread men or mince pies. The bakery is going on table nine with some artisan breads and pies and quiches, so I can slot in between you. I'll move the hand-crafted glass baubles over *there*, and then at least they'll be safe from people marauding to get to the food. Yes?' I looked at my sheet with fresh eyes and nodded. *That looked better.*

'That looks better.' Sam agreed with me, which was good. 'So — when do you want me?'

It was a perfectly innocent question, but can you blame the inner me, the one in the 'floofy dress' bouncing along to 'Troika', for making sure the Padcock me had a tongue that stuck to the roof of my mouth as everything I'd intended to say suddenly seemed suggestive and too much like a *Carry On* movie script?

'*Erruummpphhh . . . ahhh . . . yaaaaah*,' I said instead.

Sam had a good right to look at me with his eyebrows raised. I felt myself flush, horribly redly, and cleared my throat.

'You okay?'

'Yes. Sorry. Frog in my throat.' I flapped my hand at my throat to demonstrate, then coughed a little — both to give me time to think and to continue the pretence. When I'd recovered enough, I somehow managed to speak very sensibly indeed. 'I'll be setting up for the traders to take their places from 5.45, and the official start time is six.'

'That's great. Thank you.' He grinned. 'I'll see you Friday evening then. I'll get Jay to cover the pub for the night. I think it'll be nice to do something different, and he's a good chap so he won't mind. I'll see you then. I'll sort out the roads for you, I promise. I'm on it now.' And he smiled again and headed off towards the pub. I stared after him and felt my own smile blossoming across my face.

It might only be for one evening, for just a couple of hours, but it'd be nice to be working so closely alongside Sam — we could definitely have a chat, and it was always so easy to chat to him. I was looking forward to it immensely.

* * *

I would have loved that evening. Loved it unequivocally. It could have been one of those evenings I revisited in the dead of night as I snuggled under my duvet with images of Sam dancing in my head — rather than the traditional sugar plums, as one might expect.

That evening would have been amazing . . . had Belinda not turned up. According to Edie, she'd said she might 'pop along' — which was something else my friend had casually forgotten to mention to me until practically the day of the fair. When I'd challenged her, Edie explained that she'd had to rush off and do an urgent job in her graphic design business, which was why she'd forgotten to tell me Sam was having a stall. My personal opinion was that she'd been cyber-stalking Ninian Chambers instead.

Anyway, I'd been hoping Belinda wouldn't rock up. But my hopes were dashed when she turned up with a collection of scarves to sell, at ridiculously inflated prices that were clearly more suited to her London clients than to Padcock's largely cheerful community.

I say 'largely cheerful' community, as they were pretty cheerful until they reached our part of the event, where Belinda blanked the girls she'd been so friendly with and blatantly ignored the people who were just browsing.

The Padcock community wasn't so cheerful when they were faced with that. There were many, many shocked and surprised expressions at her attitude towards them. It was rather uncomfortable to witness, actually.

I couldn't help but overhear Belinda's angry mutterings to Sam as we were so close together on the stalls. Those two were squished on one table, and Sam's gin and fruit wine — which was all very delicious, take it from me and Edie who enthusiastically tasted each delicious little offering in the tiny cups Sam had brought along — had been buffeted to the side of the table to make way for her scarves.

'I just don't think they're being very supportive,' Belinda was saying, with a scowl on her beautiful face. 'I mean, they all said it was a fabulous venture. I don't know how they can say that when they clearly don't want to buy.'

'Belinda, they're your friends. Haven't they already *bought* some scarves?'

'Yes, they have. But one can never have too many scarves.' She herself was draped with quite a few. Part of me feared that she might get up and do a 'Dance of the Seven Veils' to drum up trade if she had too much of Sam's fruity wine — because the wine was not only delicious, it was pretty dangerous too, and I'd noticed she'd already had a couple of glasses of the stuff. 'Darling, these are *designer*.'

'But they're hardly Orla Kiely or Liberty,' muttered Edie, who was sitting next to me, bundled into a chunky black sweater and a tartan, belted coat. 'Or even Hermès. They're just *Belinda*.'

'What was that?' Belinda leaned across Sam as he sat back in the seat, looking hopeless.

'I said,' replied Edie, leaning forward, 'that they're hardly Orla Kiely or Liberty, or even Hermès. They are *Belinda.*' She blinked at Belinda slowly. 'And nobody has ever heard of Belinda. So, the fact you're trying to charge the villagers of Padcock £200 for a scarf is a little absurd.'

'They are a *bargain.* Versace ones are around £300. Salvatore Ferragamo ones are approximately the same price. I am targeting the same customer base. And people have heard about me. In London.'

'Okay. But I don't think the demographic of Padcock is quite the same as, say, Portobello Road. Or Notting Hill. Or Covent Garden. Or even, dare I say it, Camden Market.'

'And how would you come to that conclusion?'

Edie sniffed, then took her time answering. 'I've got a flat in Camden. I know things.' I could tell she relished every word she spoke, and I had to dip my head to hide a smile. Then Edie simply retreated into her black turtleneck, sat back in the seat and refused to engage any more.

I looked up, and, across Belinda's scarf-bedecked personage, met Sam's eyes. I raised my eyebrows and he just simply shook his head. He looked as if he'd given up.

Me, I was just quietly impressed with Edie.

Belinda sat up straighter, apparently having had a good long think. And instead of giving in gracefully, perhaps knocking some money off her scarves, maybe even smiling at people a bit more, she stood up. Then she looked around her, and, in that moment, it was very clear she'd been helping herself to more of the fruit wine, or the gin, or even both — and that she'd had *a lot* more than even Edie and I had.

She actually swayed as she stood up and then leaned on the table. 'Okay! Everybody. Listen up!' she bellowed, and we all snapped our heads around to stare at her in dawning horror. 'These scarves here — they are quite possibly the best products you'll see today at this fair! They are a brand new range from my designer collection, and are currently being sold in London. This is an opportunity for you to purchase one at a reasonable price, before they reach market value in London . . .'

And so she continued, rambling on and shouting about how good her scarves were.

'I think she's been to a few markets in London,' commented Edie quietly. 'She's just like a Barrow Boy. Intriguing.'

However, it seemed the Barrow Boy approach wasn't quite the correct one for Padcock. Everybody just sort of stopped in their tracks and looked at her. I think, actually, Veronica would have been quite within her rights to do a jolly good fist-shake right under Belinda's nose at that point.

'This is the best opportunity you'll get, outside of London, to buy these products,' Belinda shouted. 'Come on. They have to be better than anything you can buy locally!'

'*Sooooo* the wrong thing to say,' muttered Edie. Sam, on the other hand, just folded his arms and hid his face — I could see he was shaking his head, even from that position. The attitude of a man who had truly given up.

'Local? Better than anything one can buy *locally*?' came a loud, strident voice, followed by a couple of 'arfs' and 'umfs'. Mrs Pom-pom, of course. 'If I wanted London prices and London fashions, I'd go to London, my dear. I think you've misjudged the situation, somewhat.'

There was a murmur of assent, and suddenly a sea of people all nodding in agreement.

'Yes, this is a fair to support local craftspeople.'

'Mrs Pomeroy is right. This one's for Padcock!'

'Padcock needs more support than London!'

'But doesn't she live in Padcock?'

'Yes, but she clearly doesn't like it much . . .'

And so it went on, as you can imagine. It was a truly uncomfortable situation.

'Come on, Belinda.' Sam finally spoke,

his tone calming — very much the voice of reason. He stood up and tried to put his arm around her in an attempt to get her to sit down.

But she pushed him away. 'No, Sam! Get off!' She shook him off and opened her mouth to say something again, but it seemed Sam had really had enough at that point.

'Belinda. Come on. We're leaving.' His voice steel, he took her by the hand and almost dragged her out from behind the table. 'Sorry, everyone. Sorry. My girlfriend isn't herself tonight. So sorry. Please — enjoy the rest of the fair,' he called as they left. She started complaining and grumbling, and she no doubt kept it up all the way to the Spatchcock. I would not have wanted to be in Sam's shoes that evening.

On the plus side, once they'd gone, people started swarming over to our table to have a look at the scarves. I deflected them all as best I could, shoving all the scarves back into their boxes. They really were quite pretty, and I knew I wasn't folding them properly, but I wouldn't have said they were £200 worth of pretty. Regardless, I still couldn't let them be ruined. While I sorted all that out, Edie made sure the customers were more interested in the gingerbread men and mince pies we were selling, as well as the alcoholic products Sam had left behind.

'As you can see,' Edie said to someone, 'the homebrew is *pretty* potent!'

The person she was addressing ended up buying one of everything Sam had on sale.

I found out a little later it had been Veronica's mum.

★ ★ ★

The next day, when things seemed a little calmer, I took the boxes of scarves, as well as the rest of the gins and wines, back to the Spatchcock and left them on the doorstep of the pub, remembering Sam's assurances that nobody was a doorstep thief in Padcock. Later on that day, a beautiful bouquet of flowers appeared at my door, with a miniature bottle of Sam's gin tucked inside it . . . and a pair of legs below it.

'It's amazing how that bouquet knocked on the door,' I commented.

Sam was, of course, tucked behind the flowers.

He popped his head out and half-smiled. 'I think we owe you an apology. Belinda and I. Sorry for last night.'

You don't owe me an apology, I wanted to say. *She does!*

But, of course, I didn't verbalise that.

'Oh. Thanks. There's no need. Really. No lasting damage, I'm sure,' I said instead.

'I know. But you'd put so much work into it, and I — I mean *we* — really wanted to see it succeed. My home brews were a bit potent. She didn't realise. My bad.' He shrugged and the flowers wobbled and rustled. 'What I'm saying is that she didn't do it on purpose. I'm sorry.'

'It's okay. Honestly. She's probably doing so well in London that she thought Padcock would, well—' I pulled a face.

How to phrase it? 'Padcock would be the same . . . I guess?'

'Quite possibly.' He lowered the flowers slightly and looked me in the eye. 'You don't need to make an excuse for her. I know that's what you're trying to do. You're a lovely person, Cerys, you really are.' He lifted the flowers towards me again and I took them.

'Thank you, Sam. I really mean it. And Sam?'

'Yes?'

I lifted the flowers towards him, acknowledging the gesture. 'You're lovely as well, Sam.'

'Ha!' A mischievous twinkle appeared in his eyes. 'How do you know I'm not doing this to get you on-side so you'll do that gig you promised me?'

I laughed at that and shook my head. 'Because, Sam Mackintosh, I never promised I'd do a gig for you.'

'Edie said you did. Edie told me you'd promised to do it. I'm pretty sure you mentioned it to me too.'

'Nice try. But you know I didn't.'

81

Then he winked and bowed ever so politely before beginning to back away, still bowing. Then he stopped, stood up straight and pointed at me. 'One day, one day you'll do it. You will.'

I paused and then suddenly heard myself saying something I wasn't sure if I meant or not. 'You know, Sam. I actually might.'

What? Where the heck did that come from?

Sam's face changed and suddenly became serious. He walked towards me again and looked at me hopefully. 'You will?' he asked. 'Really? It would mean a lot to me if you did.'

'I'm not promising anything,' I added hurriedly. 'In that moment, I just thought I . . . might. I might *consider* it.'

It suddenly hadn't seemed such a scary thing to do — which was odd, as it had been quite scary to even think about it before that. But now — now it seemed I *could* think about it. Which was . . . lovely.

'Thanks, Cerys. I do hope you *do*

consider it. Look, have a great Christmas, Cerys, if I don't catch you on your own to tell you. And again — sorry about the Christmas Fair.'

'Don't worry about it. You too. Have a lovely Christmas, Sam.'

I watched him as he smiled one more time and turned to leave.

I watched him as he walked away, back towards the pub and Belinda.

I wondered if it was too early to open the gin.

5

Christmas Present

Fast forward to this Christmas, to 'Christmas Present' as Dickens put it so succinctly, and there I was, absent-mindedly cradling my fake baby bump in Sam's pub, residual sheepiness all around us. I was still staring up at him like the world had stopped turning and time itself had come to a halt. In that moment, I could almost imagine I had *that* sort of life. That I had Sam and a baby on the way. And, yes, a country cottage in beautiful Padcock.

But, of course, I didn't have that sort of life. And I had to extricate myself from that idea as quickly as I could.

'Oh well,' I said, falsely bright. 'Any time you need a shepherd, give me a call. I should probably get back to Edie. We've got planning to do. Yes — lots of planning.' Because, truthfully, tomorrow was

84

the Christmas Craft Fair, and we did, genuinely, need to get a few more things sorted before our stallholders arrived, and the village descended on the High Street to wassail and be merry.

But even though I knew I should have walked away and started to think seriously about the volume of gingerbread men required, I didn't move at all. I just kept standing there, looking up at him, part of me lost in a world of fantasy while my mind sorted through the muddle of this rather bizarre day — where Padcock had entertained a cast of carol singers in gorgeous, snuggly cloaks, and ice skaters and candlelight, and rosy-cheeked children bowling hoops down the street . . . and sheep had invaded our lovely pub, and I had reverted to my Border collie roots to save Lovely Sam from being indiscriminately trampled.

I blinked to bring myself back to reality and dipped my head, at last beginning to turn away from Sam.

But he grabbed my arm and it stopped me in my tracks. 'Cerys —'

'No, Sam. Don't go there,' I muttered, flashing a quick look around the pub to see if anyone was watching and had guessed what was passing between us. Which, in my case, was a whole host of emotions ranging from anger to hurt to frustration. 'I can't talk to you right now. So . . .' I pasted a fake smile on my face, to match the fake baby bump, and manoeuvred myself out of his way. It was really hard to walk elegantly with a big tummy — let me just state that as a fact right here — and that was probably why Edie was sniggering and pointing as I came back.

'Dearie me. You actually look amazingly real. You know, if anyone had said Cerys was a sturdy pregnant peasant sheep person, you'd have them believing it.'

'I'm a Victorian pauper. And I need to get changed. This isn't fun any more. And I need to plan gingerbread men.' I sat down heavily, the chair creaked, and Edie started laughing again. That was my cue to give up, so I took my bonnet off in disgust, wondering if I could also hitch up my sackcloth and untie the cushiony bump discreetly.

I wriggled and soon realised there was no way the bump was coming off without some serious manoeuvring, so I just had to sit there, feeling frumpy and furious, instead of serene and fruitful in Sam-world.

But that wasn't *quite* as bad as what happened just after that.

The door flung open again, and a tall, dark man stood there. He shook his long hair out of his face and looked around the pub. His haunted, brooding eyes drilled into everyone, resting on revellers here and there as if he was searching for someone in particular. The ladies were a bit of a-flutter at him . . . but then his gaze settled on me.

He continued to look at me for a moment before his face scrunched up and he began to cry. He actually began to do that proper snotty crying and rushed over towards me. I automatically stood up to hold my arms out to him, and I noticed a few snowflakes drift in after him — real stuff, this time, because I saw it melting on his long, black pea-coat and his black scarf — and then he halted in front of me, abruptly stopped crying and gasped. 'Cerys! Oh my *God*! Is there something you should have told me?'

Well, as you can imagine, the whole pub fell silent. They knew, of course, that I wasn't really pregnant, but it was a bit of extra drama in an already surreal evening at the Spatchcock Inn. It was, after all, full of crinolined ladies and top-hatted gentlemen, as well as the lingering odour of sheep.

'Geraint.' My voice was flat as he suddenly threw himself into my arms and started sobbing again onto my shoulder, the shock of my so-called pregnancy clearly not as important as the mire of despair he found himself in. I peered at everyone over his shoulder and smiled apologetically, whilst patting the back of a man who was a good eight inches or so taller than me. 'Have no fear. It's my brother.'

The pub, as one, subsided into less excited chatter.

'Cerys! Oh, I'm so glad I found you.'

'Geraint. Shut up and stop snotting on my costume.' I pushed him away and held him at arm's length. 'It's a *costume*. Don't worry, you're not going to be an uncle any time soon. They've been filming *A Christmas Carol* in the village. I'm going to be in it. Stealing fruit.'

'*A Christmas Carol*?' He looked at me through watery, brown eyes and sniffed again, loudly. 'What's that then?'

'Oh, for goodness sake. You know what it is.' I steered him towards the seat and indicated with a jerk of my thumb that Edie should move over so he could sit next to me. Honestly, he was three years older than me, but at times I felt as if I was at least a decade older. 'It's Dickens. Scrooge. Albert Finney, Kermit the Frog and Michael Caine.'

'Oh! *That* Christmas Carol.' He nodded and unwound his scarf. I wasn't sure what other Christmas Carol there could be, especially as we were all dressed up as Victorians, but I let it go. The thing with Geraint is that once he gets focused on something, everything else sort of fades into the background, and he's only ever half aware of what's going on in the real world. That's probably why he's such a successful classical musician now.

Once our folk group broke up, and after I'd persuaded him he needed a means of income and couldn't live on our meagre royalties forever, he'd at least had enough sense to reach out to our networks and get some gigs elsewhere. He'd been featured on orchestral CDs, played in a couple of André Rieu extravaganzas, worked on TV soundtracks and even on a couple of film scores. But he still never seemed happy. He always had a droopy look about him, and an annoyingly flicky fringe that hung in his face, which he tended to flip around mournfully as he heaved sighs everywhere like a musical version of Shelley or Keats or Byron.

I do think Alwen did a number on

him. And, yes, *here we go*. The only reason he ever trailed all the way down here to see me.

'Alwen did a number on me again,' he said and sighed in a wobbly fashion. 'I was catching up with some friends at home, and I popped over to Mum and Dad's . . .' At this point he stared hard at me, almost accusingly.

'I saw them last week to drop off Christmas presents,' I told him. 'I did tell you I was heading up, but you said you had stuff on.'

'Did I?' He looked thoughtful for a moment and did what I call his 'Byron Pose', where he stares out into the ether meaningfully as if deep in thought. I knew he was really just playing for time, which he usually does when he's been caught out for forgetting something. In this case, he'd clearly forgotten I'd said when I was going to Wales.

Anyway. It sounded like he'd been, and the parents had been gifted from both their offspring, so I motioned for him to continue.

'Well, I went this week.'

Yes. Yes, you did.

'And I saw Alwen.'

'Where did you see Alwen?'

'At the Christmas Folk Festival.' At this point, his bottom lip trembled again and I nudged Edie, who was staring at my brother in horrified fascination.

'Edie, go and get a round in,' I muttered.

'No! Because I want to watch *this*,' she shot back in a matching mutter, then jabbed her finger in Geraint's direction. 'I've never seen him go full-on 'Spurned Lover' in public! It might be *fun*.'

Geraint didn't realise what was going on, as he was being Byron-esque again, so I cleared my throat loudly. He jumped, coming back down to earth with a flip of that fringe.

'Yes.' He nodded slowly. Then stabbed his forefinger onto the table, emphasising all the syllables in the statement that followed. 'And. Alwen. Was. *There*.'

'She would be, because she's still in a folk group, with Dylan.'

'And she saw me in the audience.' He looked at me pitifully. 'And they went straight into '*Calon Lân*'.'

'And?' I didn't quite follow. We used to sing it all the time. It's a very beautiful song.

'She stared right at me when she sang about how she wanted a happy heart, an honest heart, a pure heart . . .'

'Yes?'

'So that was her telling me, right, that Dylan is the one who can give her all of those. Not me.' He shook his head despairingly. 'Not me.'

'Geraint. Has it occurred to you that the group had planned to sing that song and it was pure coincidence that she saw you then? Or that she didn't even see you as such — but just so happened to be looking at the audience at that time?'

'Cerys, I think she was sticking the knife in.'

'You're overreacting, brother.'

'And twisting it. Like *that*.' He made a twisting motion and scrunched his face up. I clocked Edie looking at him in astonishment. He could be pretty dramatic when he wanted to be, could Geraint.

I found it hard to believe that the group would have played that song purely because my brother was there. And Geraint had surely been a musician long enough to realise that you don't actually see anybody out there in the audience. You kind of zone out. Well, that's what I did anyway.

'Geraint, I love you, but there are two things we need to take away from this. Number one: it's been years since you broke up. Number two: get over it!'

He looked at me in surprise. 'She was the love of my life.'

'No, she wasn't.' I sighed.

'I have to confess, though, Cerys, I did have a liaison last Christmas.' His eyes misted over. 'I felt horribly guilty. It was the first liaison I'd had since we broke up.'

'The first . . . liaison . . . in all that time? And by liaison, do you mean you had a girlfriend? God, you talk like a Victorian sometimes. In fact. Here. Wear this.' I plonked the bonnet on his head and he didn't even flinch. Just sat there, looking ridiculous, wearing a poke bonnet and a sad face.

He shuddered at the word 'girlfriend'. 'She wasn't a girlfriend. I met her in a club. I was doing one of these open mic things with some of my music friends, and we got chatting. We had a few too many drinks. She liked my music. Said it spoke to her. Said she was trying to pick up her life after a break-up, and she just wanted to talk. One thing led to another and, well, next thing I knew I'd walked her home and she'd invited me in. You can imagine the rest.'

'So, you . . . slept with her?' I was aghast. My brother just didn't do things like that.

'There was no sleeping involved. Afterwards, I felt so guilty I told her I'd made a dreadful mistake and used her as a rebound. Then I went home . . . and rang Alwen.'

'Oh God.' I closed my eyes. 'You

drunk-called your ex?'

'Yes.' He looked miserable yet winsome under his bonnet. 'But I didn't speak to her, did I? Bloody Dylan answered the phone, so I just hung up. Not exactly surprising that I want to stay out of his way, is it?' He looked wretched; my silly, stupid, sweet, frustratingly loyal and, yes, sadly hapless, brother. Still, Alwen was a fool to dump him for our jack-the-lad cousin, and I knew that for sure — but Geraint didn't help himself at all.

'Look, that's all in the past. I'm sure nobody else is beating themselves up about it. Also, I'm assuming you've come down here to cry on my shoulder with no thought of where you'll get a bed for the night?'

'You assumed correctly.' He flushed a little. Acknowledgment of his gross stupidity. That was something, at least. 'I need to be back in London tomorrow for work, but you were the only person who would understand.' He heaved another deep, shuddering sob, and I rolled my

96

eyes. Geraint should be on the stage itself, never mind in the orchestra. I felt sorry for him and removed the bonnet. Probably just as well, because I could sense Edie convulsing with laughter next to me and muttering how she was going to pee herself any minute, and this was 'utterly brilliant, wasn't it?'

He still didn't flinch, but his hair was a bit flatter now.

'You can come back to mine,' I said. 'Or I can see if Sam has a room here at the pub. He's got a couple of B&B rooms.'

He narrowed his eyes momentarily. 'You blushed when you said Sam.'

'I did not.'

'You did.'

Why on earth did my brooding, lovesick brother suddenly choose that exact moment to start being so perceptive?

'Did not.' I folded my arms across my bump defensively.

He looked at me quizzically. 'Pretty sure you did.'

'Look, I didn't, right?' I stood up,

maybe a little too hastily; I nearly knocked Edie over as she was leaning forward, so very close to us, utterly in thrall now she'd calmed herself down. 'Are you staying with me or staying here?'

'With you if I can. But can we get a drink first? I'm emotionally drained.'

'You're emotionally something.' I patted him on the shoulder. 'I'll go to the bar. The people standing there will make way for a pregnant lady, I'm sure.'

Geraint flashed me a look. I literally saw the whites of his eyes. 'No, Geraint! I'm *acting*! I am *not* pregnant!' I said, quite crossly — and waddled over to the bar, where Sam's beautiful, beautiful smile spread across his face as he saw me approaching.

'Cerys. Thanks again for the help with the sheep. Look about before—' he started.

'What? Oh. No. No, Sam. Don't. I just want two glasses of wine, please. And my brother will have a whisky and soda.'

'He caused quite a stir when he came in there.'

Please don't try to engage me in conversation — please don't . . .

But it was no use. My mouth opened and I just started — well — engaging. Sam was, and had always been, so easy to talk to. If you didn't get distracted by his lovely eyes, or his big smile, or his general Sam-ness, that is.

'Hmmmm.' I gave up even trying and started to speak. 'My brother usually does cause a stir. Sadly, he's still pining over his ex-girlfriend who moved on with our cousin a while back. He feels guilty about having a 'liaison' — his words — with a lady in London last Christmas.' I shook my head. 'He's a tortured creative type, that's for sure.'

'It's nice for you to see him again though, I bet.'

'Yes, it is. Even though he's a miserable so and so.'

'I think some of our customers thought he was your mysterious other half, sweeping in on the snow.'

'Oh no. There'll be nobody sweeping my way. Not even my ex, who would categorically not crawl back for my forgiveness. From what I hear he's married with a child now anyway.' I glowered at nothing in particular. 'To the woman he left me for.' I transferred my glare to Sam, and the barb hit home.

'Ouch.'

'And he was incredibly selfish, even when we were together.' I couldn't stop now. 'I mean, one Christmas he decided to go on a boys-only holiday to Dublin. Why did I even stay with him after that? Why, Sam? It was quite clear it was never going to work.'

I didn't wait to hear his reply. I simply took my drinks and tried to flounce away. The flouncing didn't really work because I was encumbered by a baby bump, but the intention was there, even though I was still sort of facing the bar.

And just as I tried to flounce again, my favourite modern Christmas song came on. 'Last Christmas' by Wham!

I couldn't help it — I found myself looking back at him. Our eyes locked, and then I flushed as I realised what I'd said. 'Of course, you can't always help not being with the one you love at Christmas, can you?'

'No,' he replied, and suddenly looked a little sad. 'No, you can't.'

Because, you see, this is what happened last Christmas in Padcock . . .

6

Christmas Past

One year ago

My little Christmas tree was looking rather jolly, even if I did say so myself. He (because I had decided it was a 'he' and his name was Kristoff, like the character in the *Frozen* movie) had survived another year, which was surely a cause for celebration because I usually managed to kill all of my houseplants. Kristoff had proved he was pretty much self-managed though, and I was convinced he'd definitely grown another couple of inches.

'I swear you've grown, Kristoff,' I told him, as I put him in front of the shop door and began to wind fairy lights around his prickly green branches. I was proud to see that he had a few pinecones now as well. 'Honestly, you're such a good boy. You really have started to mature.' I'd also convinced myself that Kristoff thrived on positive reinforcement.

'Have I really started to mature? That's good to hear.' I jumped and turned, the end of the lights in my hand, and saw Sam was standing there. 'It's only taken me over three decades to do that. Not bad. Here. Let me help you with that.' He leaned over and gently manoeuvred Kristoff back into position. 'He's getting big.'

'He is.'

Sam straightened up and looked down at me. Over the last few months, I'd noticed that the usual mischievous twinkle in his eye had kind of dimmed, and it didn't look any brighter today.

'Sam? Are you okay?' I put my hand out and touched his arm — something I would do to any of my friends if they looked upset — but there was definitely a little zing that shot up through my fingers which made me jump. My heart started thumping a little faster, and I took a deep breath, trying to stop my body reacting to Sam's proximity. 'It's just you don't look very . . . happy. And it's nearly

Christmas, and you always look quite happy at Christmas. In fact . . .' I looked at him closely, and then sort of wished I hadn't made such a concentrated study of him, as it just confirmed to me what an absolutely stunningly handsome chap he was. 'You usually look quite happy most of the time. But you don't at the minute. Sorry to say that. But you don't. You've kind of lost your — well — your *twinkle*.' I held up the fairy lights to demonstrate, and at least he smiled a bit then.

'My twinkle. Yeah, that's a good way of putting it.' Then the smile slid off his face and he sort of tucked his arms in around his body. I felt miserable just looking at him.

'Anything I can do to help?' I asked.

'I hear you do pretty good cuppas in there.' His joke was touchingly pathetic; he'd sampled the coffees in the tea room plenty of times. 'I don't know if you can really help, but I think I do need to talk to someone. Sorry. Maybe now isn't a good time for you. No. Forget it. You don't need me offloading.'

All of a sudden, it seemed to grow quite dark in my little corner of Padcock. The sky had gone a peculiar grey, and, as I looked up, I felt a couple of sleety drops hit my face. *Unpleasant.*

'Honestly, Sam, I'd much rather you came inside and offloaded than we stand out here any longer than necessary. I'll flip the shop sign to closed, so nobody will bother us. And Edie isn't in, so we won't have a third wheel—' I felt my cheeks grow hot as I said that. It must have sounded terrible! 'God, I'm sorry. That came out totally wrong. Why would there be a third wheel? Why? Why would I even suggest that you and I were two wheels? I just wouldn't. I mean that sounds — that sounds . . .' My voice trailed off. 'That sounds quite bad. Sorry.'

He sort of half-smiled, but then it slipped away again. 'I'd honestly love to two-wheel with you. I really would. Yeah. Let's go inside.' He gestured for me to go first. 'After you. Will Kristoff be okay out here?'

I flashed a look at him and saw he was joking, so I shrugged. 'He's tough. He's from good northern stock. Come on.' I headed inside and he shut the door behind us whilst I tried not to blow his previous statement up into mammoth proportions. *I'd honestly love to two-wheel with you. I really would.* He meant that he'd be happy to talk. That was all. I had to remember that.

Sam took his coat and scarf off, hanging them up on one of the pegs on the wall, then followed me to the counter where I pressed a few buttons on my shiny coffee machine. Within moments, we each had a gingerbread latte in our hands. I knew he liked them — he sometimes came in for a takeaway, and it was a rather special Christmassy drink anyway. I grabbed a couple of mince pies as well and put them on a plate between us as we sat down.

It felt oddly familiar and companionable, sitting with him. Different to just sitting with a friend like Edie, or someone I was close to like Geraint. I couldn't quite explain it — but it felt right, and it felt nice, and I wanted to be able to sit with him and share a coffee every day. Preferably over breakfast.

But, of course, I couldn't ever think about that, because Belinda was there like the bloody ghost of Jacob Marley — a phantom shackled to Scrooge because of the choices he'd made in life.

Bloody Belinda.

'I think Belinda is planning to leave me.'

I jerked my head up so quickly that I almost gave myself whiplash. 'What?' It wasn't the most inspired of responses, but I was shocked, and, when I'd had time to examine my feelings a little more, I realised I was also just the tiniest bit delighted as well — which makes me sound like a really bad person, doesn't it? Or maybe it just makes me more human and relatable, depending on one's viewpoint.

'Belinda. I think she's planning to leave me. Permanently.'

'But she's in London most of the time

anyway. What makes you think she'll leave you properly?' *I mean why would you? Why would anyone want to leave Lovely Sam?*

'She says she's not really happy here. That she needs to be in the city full-time to make things work.'

'But surely loads of small businesses operate out of all over the place? She's got the Internet! She can base any meetings she needs to attend around the days she's there. She can come here at a weekend and take time off. Surely?'

'You'd think so. I mean, what you've said there is quite reasonable. I think most people would do that. Would settle for that. But Belinda's not one to settle for anything; not if there's a chance of a newer, shinier toy, just out of reach.'

'What gives you that impression? Maybe you're overthinking things. In fact, I'm *sure* you are.' I was trying to be all supportive, but part of me was pretty miffed at this new role as essentially a relationship counsellor to the only man in the world who I wished, I *desperately* wished, was single.

He looked right into my eyes then, and I deliberately clenched my hands tighter around my mug so I didn't reach up and touch him; stroke his cheek to make him feel better; move that ever-present bit of hair away from his forehead so I could see all of his face . . .

'I don't think I'm overthinking things, Cerys. More and more things are disappearing from the flat — more and more of *her* things. It's like she's doing that thing where you split your possessions up — do you know what I mean?'

I nodded slowly. 'I have three spotty mugs in my kitchen upstairs. A red one, a blue one and a yellow one. I guess the other three are in my ex's new house — if his new girlfriend allowed him to keep them. They're also red, blue and yellow. It seemed the fairest way to do it. I also have matching spotty bowls and saucers and plates. Three of each.'

'I get it. I've got half empty bookshelves up there. Half empty wardrobes. Half a cutlery set. Half a dinner set — just

109

like you.' *Oh. Now that sounded ominous.* 'We're left with the bare essentials of girly stuff in the bathroom. One shower gel. One shampoo. One conditioner. One body lotion.' He pulled a face. 'One bottle of perfume that I know she doesn't like that much. All the nice stuff is gone. I mean, correct me if I'm wrong, but if you're only going to be somewhere part time, you only need part-time possessions, don't you?'

'I'd suspect so.'

'And do you know what the worst of it is? The very worst of it?'

I shook my head. I didn't know.

'She's told me she's staying there over Christmas as business will be slower, and she can take stock of everything and plan for the future. And I wasn't even bothered when she told me. I was actually kind of glad.'

His face flushed, and I guessed he thought he'd maybe said too much — because *woah*, rewind there: *I wasn't even bothered when she told me. I was actually kind of glad.*

'You were glad?' I blinked. I had to repeat it and get it clarified, because it just sounded the most bonkers thing I'd ever heard. How could you not want to be with the person you were supposed to be in love with *at Christmas*?

'Yep.' He sat back in his seat and frowned. 'That's not great, is it? Truth be told.' He looked at me again, so intensely I felt I was rooted to the chair. 'There are other people I'd rather spend Christmas with. Other people I'd rather spend my time with. Belinda and I — well — things haven't been great for a while, but I really wanted it to work, because I felt so lucky she was in my life. I've known her for ten years, although we've only been together for five. I met her in my final year at uni — we were in some of the same lectures, and she was always the one that stood out from the crowd; she was the driven one, the one that pushed herself. She was doing Business and Marketing and was the most outgoing, confident person I'd ever met. She was beautiful and popular and I fancied her like crazy.' He smiled wryly. 'She wouldn't have anything to do with me, a sad little Business Management person, beyond a couple of drinks and a couple of kisses. But I bumped into her in Covent Garden five years ago — the Christmas before you came to Padcock, actually, and we got along well. She was still just as driven and passionate as she always had been, and I was totally besotted with her — this girl I'd been desperate to go out with all those years ago. And the next thing I knew, she was coming down here most weekends.'

'*Mmmffrffff.*' I relapsed into my usual non-committal mumblings to encourage him to continue. But once the floodgates had opened, it seemed he couldn't stop.

'But then one night, after she'd had a few glasses of wine, she told me most of her friends had coupled up and, when she'd met me again, she was starting to feel left on the shelf; was just delighted that someone was still interested in her. I asked her again in the morning whether she was just with me because of that, and she laughed and said not to be so stupid.'

'*Arrrgffffh . . .*'

'And then, somehow, she ended up moving in with me and letting her place out. She said she wanted a project and she could help me get the Spatchcock up and running even more successfully, which she did — although I told her that one of her ideas, which was to turn it into a high-end gastropub, was maybe a little too ambitious for Padcock. That was a couple of weeks before one of her uni mates had her wedding — the first of a hideous series of the damn things with one outdoing the other throughout that whole summer. So, off we went to the first wedding, and she spent the whole time saying 'we' had a 'little place in the country' and 'she' had a base in London, and how I had my own business and she was helping me to market it.' Sam's eyebrows pulled together angrily. 'God. I *have* been stupid. Very, very stupid.' He looked at me, his eyes suddenly widening in realisation. 'Do you think she just intended me to be a plus-one who sounded like I'd done exceptionally well out of life? Because that was the tale she trotted out at each event. Or was I just the next tick-box on the Gantt chart of her life? Project Sam. Someone with a business I can play with to build my CV up; someone who's grateful to have me. Tick.'

'*Ummggglll . . .*' I swallowed. How could I even speculate on Belinda's motives? 'Did — did any of the friends want to come and visit you here?'

'Yeah — yeah they did. She told them it wasn't convenient, we were getting an extension built and some work done in the grounds — in fact, I was getting the beer garden landscaped and the entrance porch redone — and they said they understood and would look forward to a 'formal invitation'. I remember we laughed about it in the car coming back, but inside she must have been thanking her lucky stars there was a good reason not to have them here.'

We locked eyes, and I noticed again

how sad he looked. 'Part of me thinks I'm letting my younger self down if I don't at least try to fight — I felt so lucky and privileged that Belinda Adams finally wanted to be with me, Sam Mackintosh, after all those years. But then . . . I think you know in your heart, don't you? As you grow up and change, and grow apart from the person you're with, or move away from the person you thought you were, you just know. And with her, with us, I just don't know any more. We've both changed from who we were at uni. And maybe it's time to cut my losses and accept it's not working out the way I'd hoped it would when I used to daydream about her all the time. So yeah. There are other people I'd *much* rather spend time with. But we were happy once. I'm sure we were.'

Wow. That was deep. But I found myself wishing I knew *who* he wanted to spend more time with. The thought made me burn up inside, and my heart was jumping around all over the place, because in my head I was the one he wanted to be with . . . So, I said the only thing I could think of.

'Another mince pie, Sam?'

7

Christmas Past

Still One Year Ago

It was the day of the Christmas Craft Fair, and we were chatting as we were setting up. It seemed the fair was going to become a bit of an annual event in Padcock now, which was brilliant; people had been asking us since October whether we were doing it again.

At that moment, we were bringing tables out to the front of the shop. Edie had painted a big banner which we'd hung across the window, and it wouldn't be long before people started turning up with things to sell. The rows of tables stretched halfway down the road, and Veronica had said she was going to get the WI to sing some carols under the big Padcock Christmas Tree at the top of the High Street. It was all going to be very festive and lovely. And snowy — we'd also had a fine dusting of snow which, strangely, put people in a good mood, and a few passers-by smiled and chatted as they passed us on the street.

But Edie couldn't hide her disgust as I relayed my conversation with Sam.

''Another mince pie, Sam?'' Edie stared incredulously at me. 'He's sitting there, with you, in a deserted building, pouring his heart out to you, sharing his deepest secrets, telling you he thinks it's over with his girlfriend, the magic of Christmas twinkling all around you, maybe even implying that he'd like to start afresh with someone else . . . and you offered him another mince pie?'

'Well, what was I supposed to do?' I scowled. 'It was just my interpretation of it. I may have been mistaken. There may not have been any of those implications *at all*. Maybe it was just wishful think-ing.'

Edie, of course, knew my feelings towards Sam. And whilst she respected the fact that he was 'in a relationship' and agreed that I shouldn't be throwing myself at him or trying to split people up, she also disliked Belinda and thought they were totally wrong for one another.

However, Edie was also pragmatic and a realist and saw the conversation I'd just had with Sam as 'cautiously quite encouraging' and an indication that not all was rosy in 'Blam-world'. But I *definitely* wanted to wait and see how things progressed on the Belinda front before I started dancing in the beer garden dressed in nothing but tinsel and fairy lights, singing 'All I Want for Christmas is You' — which was one of Edie's more far-fetched and drunken ideas.

We picked up a table in unison and began to shuffle sideways with it like crabs. 'Did Sam have another mince pie, though?' she asked curiously. I knew she would want to know.

'No.' I glared at her. 'He drained his coffee, made some excuse about having to be somewhere and practically ran out of the place.'

'It does seem as if you were 'the one' he was talking about then.' She put down her end of the table and stroked her chin thoughtfully, and I gave up.

'No.' I let my end drop with a grumpy-sounding clatter. 'It would have been nice if it was me he meant, but I think that he probably meant he'd enjoy Christmas with his friends and family more than having that sort of toxic atmosphere lingering around with the turkey dinner.'

'I'm guessing Belinda doesn't want a table this year.' Edie frowned as she moved over to straighten out a tablecloth covered with frolicking elves scampering around on it. 'Not after the carry-on last year.'

'Don't remind me.' I shuddered, remembering. 'She didn't respond to my email so, as far as I'm concerned, she can't have one. Nobody wants those stupid overpriced scarves anyway.'

'What scarves?'

I froze as I heard Sam's voice. My heart began to thump as the scenario played out in my head whereby Belinda was standing next to him and had heard me diss her products.

I turned, slowly. *Thank God he was alone*. 'Sam! Oh hello. Yes — it was someone from another village. Heather's Hand Knits or something.' I pulled a face and scowled. 'Nobody you know. She said she charged a premium for them because they were knitted from her dogs' shedded coats, and the raw product was a finite substance so . . .' I let my voice trail off and shrugged for good measure. 'Anyway. Edie's allergic to dogs and I couldn't take the risk of her sneezing everywhere.'

'Don't lie.' Sam actually smiled at me. 'I know exactly whose scarves you meant. But no. She can get more on a stall at Covent Garden for them, apparently. So that's where she is.' He cast an amused glance at Edie, who was doing a good job of ignoring us, even though I knew she could hear us perfectly well and also that I'd pay for that allergy comment at some point in the future. 'They're awful scarves anyway. Overpriced. I just wish I knew what she's planning. Because I sure as hell don't know, no matter what she says. We really need to sit down and talk. Things can't go on like this any longer.' He looked into the distance and glowered. 'She texted earlier and asked if I could send some more things to her. I've just been to the post office and sent off her hair straighteners and her Dyson Airwrap thing, along with the rest of her make-up. Next day delivery. Makes me think she's going to be doing a bit of dressing up over the next few days.'

I didn't really know how to respond to that one, so I lowered my gaze and chose not to answer.

Sam continued. 'Anyway. That's my problem, not yours. I'm just passing by to see where you're squeezing me and my home brews in this year. I'd quite like the spot I had last year please, if it's not already taken. I wouldn't take up much room. And we could team my drinks with your things if you like. On the baked goods stall. You are doing those gingerbread men again, aren't you? And the mince pies?'

I wondered if there was just a tiny bit of an emphasis on the words 'mince pies'; a subtle reminder of our conversation from the previous day.

'Oh! No — that won't be a problem. My gingerbread men will be rampant, and I can always squeeze you in amongst my goodies.'

Edie choked a little behind us and expertly turned it into a cough. I realised, too late, that my voice had come out kind of husky and there was definitely an innuendo there if Sam cared to spot it.

I also realised that Edie was still definitely listening to what we were saying.

I felt my cheeks burn up and blinked stupidly as he fought back what seemed to be a snigger. 'Thank you for allowing me to squeeze, Cerys,' he said over-seriously. 'I shall never forget your generosity. I'll pop back with the moonshine.' He made a little mock bow, stuffed his hands in his pockets and started making his way along the road.

I took a deep breath and then called

after him. 'Sam!'

He turned, surprised, and looked at me curiously.

I hurried to where he'd stopped so I was standing in front of him again. 'You know, if you're going to be on your own at Christmas, come and join me and Edie. My parents are coming, but I can squeeze you in there too.'

He smiled at me, and it almost broke my heart it was so sweet and lovely. 'Thanks, Cerys. You're a good friend. I'm going to make sure Belinda's definitely not coming home. She knows I can't really go to London because of the pub. And if she's not coming back, well, I'll go to my parents. They don't live too far away. I can be there and back between shifts. Anyway. I'd feel bad if you changed your plans for me.'

'But it wouldn't be any trouble. Really. I'd . . . *like* to spend Christmas with you.' Then I cleared my throat and pulled myself together. 'If circumstances meant you didn't have any other plans, of course.'

'Of course. I'd like to spend it with you as well. It's just —'

'I know.' I stopped him before he could justify it. I knew, of course, what it all boiled down to: a beautiful yet selfish brunette who definitely seemed to be stringing him along and plotting an escape. I hadn't forgotten her comments about an 'escape plan' all that time ago.

'I've asked her, you know?' he said suddenly. 'I've asked her what she's planning. I asked her today when she was demanding I send the package.'

'And?'

'And . . . she laughed! She said she'd be back in the New Year. And I shouldn't worry.'

'Oh. Okay.' I felt completely deflated. 'At least you know though. You might stop worrying now.'

'Yeah. I might.' He looked at me for a moment more, then sort of half-smiled, turned away and walked back to the pub.

★ ★ ★

The upshot was that Belinda didn't come back for Christmas anyway. And my Christmas Craft Fair was a far more relaxed event this time around. Sam shared our table, and yes, he may have been a little more quiet than usual, but he put a good show on.

'Is everything okay?' I asked him, when we had a lull in the proceedings. I pushed a gingerbread man over for him as a gesture of goodwill.

'Thanks, Cerys.' He picked it up and pondered it for a second. Then he bit its head off. I always think you can tell a lot about a person by the way they bite into a gingerbread man. Head first means they don't like to see things suffering. Feet first means they could be borderline psychos. Just my opinion, and probably not backed up with any scientific research.

But, regardless, I was glad to see Sam was a head-first man.

'Yeah, it's fine. I'm just wondering what the Covent Garden fair is like. I mean — can it be any better than this?' He grinned suddenly and pointed towards Edie who was haggling with someone over one of her paintings. The thing was, Edie was trying to haggle them down and tell them that it really wasn't worth what they'd offered to pay.

Veronica was leading the carol singers in a tuneful rendition of 'In the Bleak Midwinter', which, whilst an utterly beautiful song, was possibly not the sort of song to sing with a rigid and terrified smile on one's face, as Mrs Culpepper was doing right at the front of the choir. The carollers segued seamlessly into 'Little Donkey', which, depending on how much alcohol I'd consumed, had been known to make me sob with emotion. However, someone was singing completely out of key and Veronica was starting to look cross. I suspected it was Sally who owned the corner shop by the way Veronica was trying to sidestep along the line and stand in front of her.

And amidst the crowds of shoppers and browsers, Mrs Pom-pom's hat was bobbling its way around; she was shouting at the hounds who were more interested in the food stalls than the lady who was creating knitwear out of her dog's fur (yes, she *did* exist). It seemed the hounds wouldn't come to heel at all, and Mrs Pom-pom was getting more and more shouty, because she 'knew for certain that the hounds were pedigrees and their fur would be much more worthy of usage if you cared to knit with that instead of your mongrel's coat!' The dog lady, Heather from Heather's Hand Knits, was explaining coldly that her dogs were a designer fusion, which I guessed meant they were Labradoodles or a Cockapoos or something. But Mrs Pom-pom was not to be dissuaded, continuing to insist, and I quote, 'the beasts are *quite* mongrels. They were mongrels in my day and they are simply *expensive* mongrels now.'

She had a point. But the dogs who selflessly gave up their fur for the cause were beautiful animals, and undoubtedly lovely mongrels to possess. They also appeared to be getting on well with

Umbert and Arfur, which was a nice bonus.

'Nothing,' I said to Sam, looking around the village as my heart swelled with love and pride for Padcock and all its crazy inhabitants. 'Nothing is better than this.'

I turned to him, like a magnet was pulling my face towards his, and he was staring at me, and our eyes locked, and there was one of those weird moments you sometimes experience when the world goes on around you, but you don't notice a thing.

'Nothing,' he said softly. 'Nothing is better than this.'

Then Umbert — or Arfur — bumped into our table and sent an avalanche of gingerbread men flying down into the open maw of his and his brother's gobs, and the moment was lost.

Which, upon reflection, was probably for the best under the circumstances.

8

Christmas Past

Yes, it's still One Year Ago

A few days later, on Christmas Eve, my parents, Edie and I all squeezed into a corner of the Spatchcock next to the fire. Mum and Dad didn't really do pubs, but as they were my festive guests, I'd persuaded them to come along and have some mulled wine and some sherry after the carol service at the church.

'It's a kind of a 'thing', you see,' I told them, as they sat looking rather dazed in amongst an excited crowd of Padcockians. (I'm not actually sure if that's what the villagers would call themselves, but I quite like the sound of it.) 'We all do the carol concert, then come here. There's a bit more singing and some festivities, and then we go home. But there's a Midnight Mass service as well, which I've been told is good . . . but I'm usually in bed by then.'

'Cerys. This CD is rubbish. It's the same one Sam plays every year. Will *you* entertain us instead?' Edie suddenly asked.

I knew that Edie found this time of year quite difficult, what with being completely on her own. Her mum and step-dad travelled a lot, and she wasn't that close to either of them anyway.

From what she'd told me, her mum had her when she was quite young and she'd been passed around like a parcel between her mother and her gran and boarding school all her life. And I'd only ever met one friend of hers; a lovely guy called Barnaby who she knew in London. She called him Earnest Barnaby, because she said he always looked 'very earnest'. She was right.

But I digress. I was just really glad Edie was there and part of our celebrations. It was a shame Geraint wasn't there, but he happened to be working at a theatre in London over Christmas. It was a gig he'd got last minute, and I'd been a little bit huffy because it was the first time since Alwen-Gate that there would have just been our parents and us — and Edie, of course — for Christmas. My aunt and uncle were going on a cruise, which was bonkers to me — why would you want to go on a cruise over Christmas? And risk rolling waves, unfriendly weather and combine it with a huge Christmas lunch? It was a recipe for disaster — guaranteed.

Sea sickness, anyone? Another Kwell with your sprouts, madam?

Nope. No thanks.

My parents had agreed with me and Geraint that a cruise was rubbish, and so had decided to come here instead. But then Geraint had called off. I couldn't really blame him — it was a good job and good pay in one of the big theatres doing the pantomime. It had solved the accommodation problem anyway — I've only got two bedrooms, and my parents would have been in the spare room, so my brother would have had to sleep on the sofa.

However, Edie was now suggesting that I entertain the hordes in the pub, which hadn't been my plan at all.

'Edie, it's the same CD he has every year because it's a good Christmas CD. There are only certain songs you *have* to hear each year, and this has them all. There's no need for any others. I mean, this one's a classic.' It was 'Winter's Tale' by David Essex, and say what you will, the man still had it. Mum was already swaying dreamily along to it, but Dad was more of a Slade man — you wouldn't think it to look at him, but he had been known to get up and bop when he'd had too much sherry.

'Will Wham! be on this?' Mum asked. 'I do like a bit of George Michael.'

'Which bit, eh?' Dad nudged her and smirked and Mum blushed, but before she could say something saucy about his bum in the 'Faith' video, I interrupted.

'Yes, Mum. It's on after this one. Listen. It's coming on now.'

'Oh good.' Then she looked at me like a cheeky, middle-aged elf and smirked. 'I can listen to that while you set up then.'

'What? I'm not setting up anything!' I was horrified. 'Anyway, I can't. My guitar is at home, and Geraint is in London. I don't do solo shows. And I haven't performed in ages. So, no.'

'Yeah, you're doing *all* that tonight, my love.' Edie cackled and slid out of her seat. She hurried over to the bar, her stubby blonde ponytail decorated this evening with tinsel, and rapped on the counter until Sam noticed her. He smiled at her and they put their heads close together, then he grinned and ducked down behind the bar. When he popped up again, he was holding my guitar. He passed it across the bar to Edie, and as she came back with it, holding it above her head and shaking it in triumph, he switched the CD off, just as George Michael breathed the last few sultry notes of 'Last Christmas'.

'She stole it! She *stole* my guitar from my house!' I pointed at Edie who didn't look guilty in the slightest.

'She had a little help,' said Dad,

patting my knee. 'We haven't heard you play in so long, and we were *more* than happy to help arrange it.'

Great. My parents had also betrayed my tiny trust. All of them were actual facilitators in the grisly crime of guitar-napping.

'Ladies and gentlemen!' shouted Sam. Like magic, the hordes shut up and looked expectantly at him. 'We've got a treat in store for you tonight. I'm wondering how many of you know that our Cerys is a musician?'

There was an interested rumble, and a few shaking heads and a couple of 'no, no I didn't!' sort of comments going around the room like a Mexican wave.

'Well, she is — and she's agreed to do some songs for us tonight.' A slurred, drunken sort of cheer went up, and I just knew my face had gone beetroot as everyone looked over at me; some people even gave me a thumbs up or started clapping.

'I really haven't prepared anything . . .' My voice came out all quavery and pathetic. 'Really.'

'Then just do some of the songs you usually do,' suggested Dad. 'If they're in Welsh, nobody will know if they're Christmas songs or not, and they'll all sound great.'

'But . . .'

'Ah, Cerys. We've come All This Way to hear you.' That was Mum, putting on her best sad-and-disappointed voice, yet also managing to sound as if she was Speaking With Capitals.

'You haven't. You've come All This Way to spend Christmas with me and gobble up a turkey lunch.'

'Gobble!' giggled Edie. 'Like a turkey!'

I glared at her.

'Edie Brinkley, this is All Your Fault.' *See, I'm my mother's daughter and can also Speak With Capitals.* 'I can't believe the three of you planned this behind my back.'

'Four,' said Mum. She handed me over a neatly folded piece of paper. 'Geraint suggested some songs for you.'

Automatically, I unfolded the paper

and scanned the list. He'd made some good choices, although it pained me to say it. 'There's no getting out of this, is there?'

'Nope.' Edie smiled at me.

I looked at the potential audience, who were still staring expectantly at me, and felt my cheeks heat up even more. I gave the potential audience a little wave. They waved solemnly back as one. 'Just some technical issues!' I said in a squeaky little voice. 'Be with you all soon!' They nodded and watched even more expectantly as I tried to get my head into the game, as they say.

I refolded the paper and hissed at Edie. 'Edie — this is the equivalent of you not painting, okay? And me forcing you to do it by arranging something sneakily.'

My friend had the grace to blush and look down. 'I do paint,' she muttered.

'Not the stuff you should be painting. You do stuff for the craft shop and the village. It's all commercial. It's not from the heart. You're worth more than my Padcock postcard stash.' I'd seen what she was capable of — she'd proudly shown me the art exhibition catalogues she'd been lauded in — but it seemed, to my amateur eye at least, that since her gran died, she'd lost her way; lost the spark that made her art incredibly amazing and abstract and so very 'Edie'.

'That's my choice. And anyway, I'm *happy* doing Padcock postcards.' She looked furious, and I knew better than to push it on Christmas Eve — but I wouldn't forget it.

'Okay.' I sighed and looked around again at the Spatchcock crowd. My heart was thumping and I felt incredibly nervous. I truly hadn't performed for years — not since I'd come to live here, because strumming in an empty room thinking about a Lovely Sam you've only just met obviously didn't count. And besides that, Rhys had managed to squash any delight I felt at playing my guitar. Just before we'd broken up, whenever I'd picked it up in the music room and begun to play, I'd hear him slam the door of whichever room he was in, or turn up his playlist or the TV show he was watching to drown it all out. I'd been perfectly aware of his opinion of me and my music — but it was still unutterably sad that he'd felt he had to express that opinion in the way he did.

I knew that by this point, I should have been able to let go of my inhibitions and pick it up again; I had to some extent. But playing in front of people was something different.

What if someone got up in the pub and just walked out, slamming the door behind them? Even if that did happen, and it genuinely was just because it was that someone's bedtime, I'd still feel it was my fault, and by default that I'd let Sam down. Because wasn't he entrusting me to perform something of a little Christmas concert here, perhaps as a way of retaining customers for that crucial 'one more drink'?

I looked over at Sam, and he was smiling that lovely, wide smile of his, and my heart started pounding. But I knew it was more because he was smiling that lovely, wide smile of his than the fact I was about to perform a completely unrehearsed show in front of my entire village . . .

I stood up and picked up the guitar, then walked over to where he was. He came out from behind the bar carrying a stool. I shot a look at Edie, who shrugged and looked blank, but I knew she'd told him to set that up as well.

'Talk amongst yourselves, guys!' called Sam, treating the audience to another smile. 'I should have sorted a seat for her earlier. My bad. You just can't get the staff these days!' But because he was so Lovely, the audience chuckled and did just that — and then I realised that he had, again, demonstrated just how Lovely he was to *me* by directing the attention right away from us and our impromptu arrangements for a minute so I could pull myself together and get settled in position. I felt myself fall in love with him a little harder — if that was even possible.

'Thanks for doing this,' Sam said in a

low voice. 'Is this okay? I just thought, you know, you're so bloody good and you don't seem to have any confidence in your playing, so it was the only way we could do it. I'm not the only one responsible — we all were . . . You've probably guessed that now. But I've heard you. I found a CD online that your folk group recorded — you can find anything on Google, you know? Anyway. Your voice — your songs — your playing. Cerys, you are *amazing*. Really and truly.'

He indicated the stool and I nodded like a robot. 'Sure. Whatever. And thank you — for what you said there about my playing. And my singing. Thank you. Yeah. But you do know, though, that I haven't done this for ages? I don't even know what I'll be like on my own. I've always had at least Geraint with me — more often than not, I had Alwen and Dylan there as well.'

'Edie said she's heard you playing and singing as well and, to quote her, 'Cerys is quite incomparable. She's like a really,

really cool female Bob Dylan. But that's me comparing her, isn't it, and I just said she was incomparable. Hmmmm'.' I bit back a laugh at that. It was so very, very Edie. Then Sam continued. 'We all thought it was just what everyone needed tonight. You. Here. With us all.'

'No sign of Belinda coming back then?'

He shook his head. 'She's sticking to the New Year story, so we'll see. I'm just going to enjoy tonight and tomorrow as best I can. I've got my parents tomorrow, and you here tonight, so . . .' He shrugged and smiled, and my heart flip-flopped again. 'Things could be much worse. It's not a lot of fun for Belinda on Christmas Day here anyway. I'm usually in the bar. Can't blame her really.'

'I'd rather be with you in the Spatch-cock than on my own in a mews house in London.' I couldn't help it; I just blurted it out. Then we stood there and stared at one another for what seemed like ages as I wondered if I'd gone too far.

'Thing is, Cerys. I'm not sure she *is*

alone.'

And that threw yet another spanner in the works.

I mentally gave myself a shake. 'I'd better start.' I indicated the stool and Sam nodded.

Then he leaned in as if he was adjusting the stool for me and whispered, 'Cerys, I actually think I'd rather *you* were in the Spatchcock as well.' Then he frowned and sort of looked embarrassed before loping off to the bar.

So, I wasn't the only one who had possibly said too much . . .

Anyway, I won't bore you with a detailed account of my mini-concert. I do have to say, though, that the songs Geraint had suggested were perfect. They were mainly old ballads and folk songs; things I could carry on my own. As I sang, the pub fell quiet and, when I ended my last song, you could have literally heard a pin drop.

What I *did* hear wasn't a pin — it was Edie suddenly beginning to clap, and a funny noise that sounded like a disguised sort of snotty sob from Veronica. That last folk song must have made her feel emotional, even though it was actually just a Welsh version of 'The Twelve Days of Christmas', and I'd simply slowed it down and looked serious while I did it. It's called 'The Parrot on the Pear Tree', if you're interested.

I really hoped Veronica would never find out.

It could have been worse; Geraint and I had been known to do a duet about a dead pigeon. Truth.

I looked around the room, sort of in a bit of a daze. I was buzzing inside — but very deep down, because I had to maintain my serious face for effect before I slid off the stool and took a bow, just as naturally as I always had done. I had to stop myself from holding my hand out to Geraint though, as I was also used to doing. Even Mum and Dad were on their feet cheering.

'Cerys!' cried Dad. 'Wasn't that last one —'

'Yes, Dad!' I shouted back, glancing

at Veronica, who was delicately dabbing her eyes with a paper napkin. 'That's the traditional Christmas one we always end with.' I widened my eyes and nodded discreetly in Veronica's direction, and, amazingly, he got the hint.

'Ohhhh! Yes. Yes, of course. I thought it was.' And he grinned, nodded and kept clapping — *and*, I noticed, downed the rest of his sherry when he thought nobody was watching.

'That was amazing. Thanks, Cerys.'

I turned and faced Sam. He was looking down at me, his eyes shining with something I'd like to call 'love' but was probably more 'respect'. Although there was also something in his expression that looked distracted and sad; a bit haunted even, like he'd had bad news and was trying to hide it.

'No problem. I actually enjoyed it. I messed up a couple of times, but I don't think anyone noticed.'

'Nobody noticed at all. I'm stunned. I didn't realise that we had such a talented performer in our midst.'

'I sound better when I'm with Geraint.' I shrugged. It was a fact.

'Stop putting yourself down. When you get a compliment, you should say 'thank you'. It's better for you, and it's better for the person who compliments you. Now. Let's try that again. I didn't realise that we had such a talented performer in our midst.' He looked at me expectantly.

My mouth worked as I fought against the words I really wanted to say, but I managed in the end. 'Thank you.'

'Much better.' He reached out and squeezed my shoulder. It was sort of chummy and sort of familiar — and also sort of heart-breaking because it was sort of chummy and sort of familiar, but the sensation of his fingers through my thin, black, lacy dress (now I was glad they'd all persuaded me to 'dress up a bit more, *cariad*, it's Christmas Eve') made me shiver, and it wasn't from the cold. I wasn't sure if he'd felt anything, but from the look on his face, and the way his fingers kind of tensed up and stayed on my shoulder longer than was necessary, I guessed perhaps he had.

'Cerys, do you fancy going to Midnight Mass?' he asked all of a sudden, then blushed. 'It's the only time I'll get to see you properly. And I really need to talk to you. I'll kick everyone out of here at eleven and we'll have plenty of time.'

'Sure.' We did that corny thing of staring into one another's eyes while the hustle and bustle of the pub went on around us, and, for me at least, the world just sort of faded.

I hoped — I *really* hoped — that my Christmas wish from the previous year was on the verge of coming true . . .

9

Christmas Past

One Year Ago. Well . . . a lot happened that year.

My Christmas wish. Yes — I know what you're thinking. 'Why is she wishing that Lovely Sam would find himself single this Christmas?'

Well, newsflash, I'm not an angel. Much as I'd like to be an angel, there is a genuine demon that sits on my other shoulder and runs Sam-like scenarios by me every so often. In the scenarios, Sam is always single, and it's not complicated, and we can just get together. That's it. That's all there is to it.

But then real life intrudes, and Belinda comes into the tea room and brays with her mates or, worse, sits and looks down her nose at the contents of my shop whilst nursing a black coffee and doing 'work' on her laptop, sucking up my free

WiFi and making that one coffee last all morning.

I'd noticed recently that her screen-saver was a picture of her and her friends out on the town — and it wasn't our town, as we don't have a nightclub and no pubs beyond the Spatchcock, so goodness knew where it was — all in tiny body-con frocks and with perfect, Kate Middleton-esque bouncy blow-dries, waving glasses of champagne in the air.

I wondered whether that was the kind of life she wanted, rather than the reality of living in a flat above the village pub.

Anyway, my Christmas wish fluttered around my heart, hidden behind my thick woollen sweater — I'd changed by then into something a bit more suitable for walking to the other side of the village and sitting in a potentially chilly church — and I made my excuses to my parents and Edie. It had been surprisingly easy — Edie was heading home anyway and my parents were tired, so after we'd had a cuppa together, they more or less went straight to bed once we'd got back from the pub.

I met Sam inside the bar as he was locking up. The door was ajar, and, assuming it had been left like that for me, I just walked in.

The Spatchcock had a completely different feel to it with nobody around. The lights were still twinkling on the tree, but the scent of the pine needles was much stronger when it wasn't contending with perfume plus wine and real ale. The fire was low, and it wouldn't be long before it was out altogether. But more than that, there was a sort of warm silence hanging over it, and you could just imagine the old building settling down for the evening and relaxing. Sam was moving around the tree, half-hidden in the shadows near the fireplace, the embers casting the angles of his jaw and his cheekbones into sharp relief. I could have stared at him for hours.

But then he must have sensed that I was there and he looked up. 'Hey, Cerys.' He smiled. 'Let me just switch these off and I'll be with you.' He indicated the fairy lights on the tree.

'No, leave them if you can. It's so lovely in here, isn't it?' I commented and Sam nodded, then moved away from the tree. He looked around him as he grabbed his coat and scarf.

'It is. I suppose I'm just used to it. Sometimes, I'll have a coffee down here on an evening and just enjoy the silence and the last of the fire.' He shrugged. 'It's kind of better than sitting upstairs on my own. Is that weird?'

'Not weird at all. Look. We don't have to go to Midnight Mass. We can stay here or just take a walk, you know? If you want to — well — talk — then isn't it better to do it away from everyone?'

'You're right.' He frowned. 'I think, if it's okay with you, we'll go for a walk? It's a bit more neutral territory. Shall we go along by the canal? Is that all right?'

'That's fine. I love the canal.' I often wandered down there and watched the narrowboats manoeuvring along the old waterway. One of the older men who lived on a boat and often came our way called himself a River Gypsy, and I loved that term. He'd also grinned at me and said I was a 'gongoozler', which I also loved. It meant I was a person who liked to watch the boaters, and I didn't dispute that.

'Great. Come on then. Will you be warm enough?' Sam looked at me, and I nodded. As well as my chunky sweater, I had on skinny jeans, winter boots and a big coat. It was nice that he'd checked though, I thought.

Honestly, what was there not to like about this man?

Oh yeah. The fact he had a girlfriend.

'Come on then.' He indicated the door and we headed out. The coldness outside took my breath away after being in the warmth of the pub. The sky was inky black and the stars were millions of diamond pinpricks up above us. The more I looked, the more stars I could see appearing. The moon was almost full, and there was already a covering of frost on the ground.

'It would be perfect if it snowed,' I

mused.

'Then we wouldn't see the stars.'

'True.'

We fell into step, and I was aware that the fizzing between us could very well result in the creation of a new galaxy.

We chatted easily on our way to the canal, talking about the customers in the pub and how the Craft Fair had gone and my mother's shameful lusting over George Michael. I also confessed about the parrot song, and Sam laughed and said he wouldn't tell anyone. It gave me a lovely, squishy feeling inside, knowing that we were sharing a secret together.

But I was sure there was something else bubbling just under the surface as well. It hung there like a sparkling, frosty mist between us, but I told myself not to build my hopes up in case I was completely wrong. As we started to walk along the towpath, I tried instead to think about the people who were all tucked up in their little canal boat bunks, and how sweet and cosy the lit-up windows on the boats looked. I noticed the decorations and the fairy lights, and saw the tiny Christmas trees on the roofs and on the decks — and then Sam suddenly stopped under an old-fashioned street lamp that illuminated the towpath and turned to face me. It was so cold, I could see the breath misting in front of his face as he puffed his cheeks out and exhaled in a bit of a wobbly fashion.

'So. Cerys. I don't want to drag this out. Although I guess I have, sort of, because I haven't talked about it all the way along here. And that's quite draggy.'

I nodded carefully. I knew it wasn't appropriate if I agreed or disagreed. I had to fight the urge to speak and just let him talk.

'*Hrmphhphh*,' I said.

It was always really hard for me to fight the urge to speak.

'You okay?' He frowned.

'*Ummmffrrrt.*' But I nodded so he knew I was.

'Okay.' It was Sam's turn to nod and I fought down the next urge, which was to make another silly noise. 'Good.' Sam sighed and another one of those misty breaths danced through the air. 'I got a text from Belinda tonight.'

'*Ooohuphha.*'

'She wants to break up.'

'*What?*' I couldn't help myself. I had to respond to that one with a recognisable word.

'Yes. I read it just as you'd finished singing. During the applause. I glanced at the phone and saw it, and then I had to read it properly. It kind of comes up with the first few lines of the message on the screen. Otherwise, I wouldn't have read it. I'm sorry I was looking at my phone during your applause.'

'No. No, you had to. If it was something like that, you needed to read it. I would have done the same.'

'Thanks, Cerys. Here — it's right here. Just so you know I'm telling the truth.' He looked really earnest then; almost as earnest as Earnest Barnaby. He fumbled around and pressed the buttons on the phone and held it out to me.

I didn't take it though. 'Why do I need

to see it?'

'Like I say — so you know the truth. Please?'

Half-reluctantly — but only half, because I knew this could mean a world of difference to Sam and I, and what we did going forwards — I took the phone and read it. I felt my eyes widen in disbelief. There it was, in clear, precise English; not a shred of evidence of a drunk, regrettable text. It said:

I can't let this drag on until the New Year. I won't be coming back. I had no intention of doing so, but I was trying to let you down gently. However, it's gone beyond that now and I want this sorted. My life is in London and, to be frank, I don't think there's anything left for me in Padcock. There's nobody else involved. I just want out. I don't love you any more and I haven't for a while.

'Wow.' I stared at the words. 'That's harsh. Harsh, harsh, harsh.' I handed the phone back to Sam, my hand shaking a little. It brought back memories of my split from Rhys, which hadn't been sunshine and unicorns at all. 'What are you going to do?'

'I haven't answered.' He looked at the phone again, shook his head and put it in his pocket. 'My honest answer? I don't know. Part of me says it's not worth fighting for it because it's really not the same any more. But part of me thinks I need to speak to her.'

'You definitely need to speak to her. Sam, I don't like Belinda and she doesn't like me, but she's your girlfriend and you must have loved her once.'

'I know. I did. I'm just in shock. And you know what else?' He fixed his eyes on mine and my heart began to beat a little faster. 'I felt numb. I honestly felt numb. Shocked and numb — but also, a bit of me was bloody glad. Because if we split up properly, then I can move on instead of feeling like we're heading towards an inevitable train wreck. Like ripping a plaster off instead of peeling it away little by little and feeling a new pain every time. I wanted to tell you, Cerys, because — well — I think you know why.' He reached out and took my hand. He looked at it for a moment and frowned. 'Wow. This is so hard. I can't really say this without sounding like a git. I really like you, Cerys. Over the time we've known each other, I've come to like you more and more. I honestly think that if I let myself go, I would fall for you. Big time. But it's not fair on you for me to ask you to get involved with me until all this is resolved. I don't love her any more either. But I need to speak to her — I can't let it end via text. I think I'm asking you to give me some time. Not—' he added hurriedly, looking back at me, his eyes all dark and concerned '—that I'm asking you to hold on until I get this sorted. I quite understand if you want to tell me to eff off or shove me in the canal or string me up with the fairy lights. But if there's an outside chance you could, maybe, let me sort myself out, let me get this mess under control — then I'm asking if we could maybe, perhaps, give it a go? If you feel the same, of course.'

I think my mouth opened and shut like a fish's for a bit. My head was spinning and I couldn't even formulate an answer. So I nodded, a little too vigorously, took his other hand in mine — and then, before I really knew what was happening, we closed the gap in between us and we were kissing.

And it was magical.

The magic was only broken by a crash from a nearby boat which sounded very much like a pan falling off a bench. It made us both jump, and we pulled away from each other, no doubt both looking very startled indeed.

My lips were burning and tingling all at the same time, and my body was firing sensations around to places I hadn't even realised existed.

In retrospect, it was probably good that the pan crashed and disturbed us, or we may have just simply rolled onto the deck of the nearest narrowboat and lost our dignity right there and then.

'Wow.' I stared at Sam. 'I'm sorry. That doesn't usually happen when a guy tells me he's trying to sort out a complicated situation and we kind of agree not to get involved too soon.'

'Hmm. I don't think you actually answered that point though, did you?' An embarrassed sort of smile was playing around his mouth. 'I'm just as guilty as you are.'

'Hush.' I put my fingertips on his lips and shook my head. 'Stop it. *You're* excused. Let's just agree to disagree.' I removed my finger and, very reluctantly, took a step back. 'You make some fair points though. But this is Christmas, and we're allowed a Christmas kiss. That was ours. We won't kiss any more until the New Year, when we know what's happening. You need to sort things out with Belinda, and depending on which way it goes, well . . .' I sighed. This was the most magnanimous thing I'd ever said, and I hoped it would bring lots of good karma my way. 'We'll decide what to do then. If you decide to give it another go with her, I'll respect that. There's not much else I can do, really. At least I'll know for sure.' I shook my head and looked up at him, committing his face and the way his scarf was tucked under his chin, and the way his hair was all messy and tousled to my memory. I realised our kiss was probably some of the reason his hair was so messed up, actually. 'I've spent the last four years waiting for this moment, I truly have. But that's all it might be. A moment. It's Christmas Eve, I've just sung some pretty deep love songs in the pub —'

'And one about a parrot.'

'*And* one about a parrot. Why did I even *admit* that to you ten minutes ago? And you've had a hideous text. Let's just take it one step at a time. I can wait a little longer.'

'Cerys . . .'

'Sshhhh.' I shook my head and shoved my hands in my pockets. 'No. We do this *after* Christmas. When you know what's happening.'

'You're right. I know you're right.' He looked out across the dark canal and sighed. 'But yes. We should wait. This isn't fair on you. I should never have said anything. Like I said, I'm a git.'

'No,' I said softly. 'It's Christmas. It's a special time of year. We all do crazy things at Christmas. And anyway — listen.' I pointed in the direction of the church, where the bells were ringing out for midnight. 'It's Christmas Day already. All that happened yesterday. We've moved on one day already. Let's just see what happens.'

'Okay.'

'Okay.'

'But can I kiss you again? For Christmas Day, and all that?'

'Go on then. Just because it's Christmas Day.'

And so we did, and it was lovely. Not as impassioned as the first one — we took our time over it this time. I think we both knew it would be the last one for a while.

And as Christmas turned into that weird 'Twixt-mas' sort of time between Christmas and New Year, where you exist solely on leftover party food, stodge and cheese — so much cheese — I hugged the details of Christmas Eve to myself, not even telling Edie about it. I went swanning into The Spatchcock, the day after Boxing Day and Sam and I, like a pair of conspirators, both pretended nothing had happened.

There were a few secretive sorts of looks and blushes — okay, those were from me, directed at Sam when I didn't think he was looking, but that wasn't unusual so Edie didn't pass comment — and then it was New Year's Eve, and Sam and I had a New Year's kiss and a hug as everybody in the pub did at midnight. The only difference being he whispered in my ear, 'I can't wait until we can do this on a more regular basis.'

'Me neither,' I whispered back.

But then, the day after New Year, it all started falling apart.

On the second of January, nine days after we'd had our heart to heart on the towpath, I was idling away some time, peering out of my window over the rooftops of Padcock and staring longingly towards the Spatchcock — I'd found there was a certain corner of the spare bedroom I could see the front door of the pub from, if I leaned in a little bit when looking out the window.

I was nursing a cup of coffee and beginning to make plans to open the tea room again. It was my thinking that people were probably ready for a nice cuppa and a piece of cake to kind of get back to normality, or looking to enjoy a treat after a wintry walk around the village.

But then I saw her.

A taxi pulled up and Belinda got out. The driver immediately began unloading a whole load of luggage. Then Sam came out of the pub and just stared at her. There was a couple of metres between them, and she was the one to move forwards and hold out her arms to him.

Sam folded his. Then when the taxi drove away, she stood there and talked to him, then he raised his hands up and put them on the top of his head. He just stared at her and didn't move, and she leaned down to pick up a case. But then he was there, moving towards the case, picking it up. She followed him into the pub, and he came back and retrieved all the rest of the luggage before shutting the door.

And my coffee got cold as I remained standing there for, I don't know how long, in that same position, just staring at the closed door of the Spatchcock.

The tea room opened late that day.

Then, after an awful shift, where I had to be happy and smiley and welcome my customers back whilst my mind screamed *What the hell is going on?*, Sam came in at closing time, looking like — excuse the language — proverbial shit.

Thank God Edie was still a little fragile after New Year; I'd sent her home early, so I was alone when he turned up.

My heart began to pound and I hovered uncertainly between the counter and the door, not sure really where I wanted to be. But he didn't even give me time to ask the question. He just walked in, checked the tea room was empty, and flipped Edie's hand-painted sign to 'closed'.

'She's come back,' he said. 'She thinks

she could be pregnant . . . and it's mine.' His face was pale and his eyes were red, and I think he may have been a little more upset than he let on. His hair was a mess and all I wanted to do was to move towards him; close the gap and feel his arms around me again, feel my cheek against his shirt, his chin on the top of my head, and his warm body pressed against mine —

But instead, I just kept standing there, staring at him stupidly, the tears running down my face, as I felt the last hope of ever getting together with him disappear.

I nodded. 'Okay,' I said. 'Thanks for letting me know.'

I didn't even offer him my congratulations. I couldn't be happy for them, I just couldn't.

'And that text message,' he said. 'I just thought you should know. Apparently, a man came onto her in a bar. She said she wasn't interested, and he took her phone and sent me that message.'

If that's what she says, I wanted to reply. But I didn't. I just remained silent, biting my bottom lip and trying to redirect the utter pain of heartbreak and rapidly shattering dreams by picking at a stray thread on my gingham apron. The hem was unravelling. A lot like me.

But Sam continued, and it got worse. 'It's my baby, Cerys. We haven't been — close — for a while . . . but there was one time, at the beginning of December. We argued, then we got upset, then we started reminiscing over stuff . . . sorry. You don't need to know that, you really don't. We both realised afterwards it was a mistake to try and fix things that way, but there you go. I have to support her. I have to be there for her — for both of them. I have to try and make it work for that reason. And she's letting the mews house again. She says this time she's definitely going to start saving the rental. For when the ba—'

Then I finally held up my hand to shut him up. 'No. Stop it, Sam. I don't need to hear it.'

When he left, I ripped all the Christmas decorations down in the shop and shoved them back into storage. They weren't cheerful any more. They looked sad, and lonely, and tired . . . and Christmas had passed, so what was the point?

10

Christmas Present

After Belinda's bombshell, the previous Christmas had suddenly seemed not very Christmassy at all. It had hurt. It had hurt a great deal, and it took me a long time to accept that 'Blam!' looked as if it was there to stay, and the relevant parties of 'Blam!' now had a very good reason to try and put their differences aside and make it work.

I, on the other hand, decided that the best course of action during that time was to stay away from the pub. In fact, I went to my parents' house for an extended post-festive visit. They were a bit startled — I don't think they thought they were going to see me so soon after Christmas.

Geraint turned up as well, so we had a sort of second Christmas lunch. However, lovely as it was, both Geraint and I sat with miserable faces on us the whole time, and I'm sure the parents were pleased to eventually see the back of us.

Edie, who had been in charge of my little dominion, had left the craft shop in a state of genteel chaos, so sorting all that out kept me busy after I returned, and I managed to make lots of very valid excuses not to go to the pub.

In fact, I managed to avoid the Spatch-cock, Sam — and Belinda — for ages. I managed to avoid them for three whole months. Because it almost seemed that I'd blinked, and, suddenly, there we were in March. And then one day during that month, for the first time in ages, Belinda came into the tea room with her laptop in tow, and I felt absolutely sick. No way did I want to serve her.

But then she took her coat off, smoothed down her tight T-shirt, slid her skinny-jean-clad legs under the table . . .

And there was no sign of a baby bump at all.

None. Not even the suggestion that she'd had a big lunch and was a little bloated.

Now I knew that, technically, if she'd fallen pregnant at the beginning of December, which is what she'd told Sam, it was a possibility she might not be showing very much — but I couldn't even stay in the same room as her to ponder her non-existent bump.

'Edie,' I said, heading into the kitchen, where my friend was half-in, half-out of the back door smoking a cigarette she thought I wouldn't notice. 'Do you mind watching the tea room for me? I need to nip out.'

'Oh! Sure. Yeah. Of course.' She stepped outside, dropped the cigarette butt and ground it out with the heel of her biker boot. She wandered back into the tea room and I slipped outside. I wasn't really going on an errand. I knew I'd end up just walking around for a bit, but I hoped that by the time I got back, Belinda might have finished her coffee or whatever and left.

But Fate was not kind to me. I was just heading through the little narrow passageway between my shop and the house next door when I noticed Belinda scurry out of the tea room and huddle on the corner, pressing her phone to her ear just as I popped out of the gap.

There was a moment where we both stared at one another, then she spoke into the phone. 'Give me a minute, honey. I'll ring you back.'

As one, we both turned away from each other. She hurried back into the tea room, and some sixth sense told me she'd gone into the loos to take this clearly 'private' phone call. Before the sensible part of my brain could kick in and tell me not to torture myself with it all any more, I turned around and hurried back into the kitchen. We had a little staff room, which was probably the original scullery of the building, and we'd put a couple of sofas in. It was a good place for Edie and I to have our breaks — or, in Edie's case, sometimes a little nap — but it was also an excellent place to overhear conversations in the loo; of which, surprisingly, there were many.

Therefore, masochistic-me held my breath and pressed my ear to the wall.

'Hiiiiiii!' I heard. 'God, Jools, I'm sooooo glad to hear from you. I swear I'm going mad here. It's so bloody *dull*! I literally cannot wait to get back to London this weekend. What? Oh, hell yes. I *fully* intend to get hammered.'

Hammered? Did she mean drunk? I stood up straighter and frowned. *You shouldn't be getting hammered* or *drunk when you're pregnant.*

And then she laughed, that awful silky laugh that was as fake as she was, and I could imagine her running her fingers through her long, dark hair. 'I know! Thank fuck for false alarms, yeah? But I'm soooo pissed off I didn't wait until I was sure before I let the house go to those tenants though. I guess I just panicked, but at least he believed it was his. So halle-bloody-luljah here I am, stuck in the bloody countryside when I could be back home. It's *really* not all it's cracked up to be, living out here in the sticks. What? Oh yeah, he knows it was a false alarm but I'm kind of screwed without the mews house anyway, to be honest, so I need to stay here for a bit regardless. You know, when I saw everyone having babies, I thought it was something I should do too — but, to be honest, it came close that time and I really wasn't happy about it . . .'

Then they started general chit-chatting, and I continued standing there, frozen to the spot.

It seemed there was no baby on the way, and she was pretty happy about that.

And it also seemed that, once the imminent danger of her having a baby had passed, she was happy to just pick up from where she'd left off — travelling back and forth to London as the fancy — or the business — took her. And all the time, she was keeping Sam hanging on here. I just *knew* that she'd be off again as soon as she could, spending more and more of her time in London and expecting Sam to basically put her up and support her.

And, worse than that, she didn't really want babies with him anyway. Which was anathema to me, because, if I was honest with myself, it was the one thing I desperately wanted. And that comment about him believing it was his? Well, it could be interpreted either way: like he trusted her when she was away, so of course he would believe her . . . or could she have slept with someone else, thought she was pregnant a few weeks later and bolted home to hide her mistake?

But, despite all of these revelations, I knew it wasn't my place to say anything to Sam.

And it made me feel very sad.

★   ★   ★

Their strange relationship rumbled on. And still I stayed away from the pub. I now had another reason to avoid the place — I couldn't bring myself to face him, not when I knew she was basically using him. That was unforgiveable. As my mum would say, she wanted to have her cake and eat it. She wanted Sam lingering here for her, and the life she craved in London ready to absorb her again. I was certain that she'd go back on a more permanent basis before too long.

But it seemed the Fates were against me yet again, because one day in April the bell above the door rang, and I turned around from the coffee machine with a smile on my face . . . and saw Sam standing there, looking uncomfortable.

'Hello, Cerys,' he said. 'Long time no see. Surprising in a village of this size.'

'Very surprising.' I tried to sound neutral, but my heart was pounding, and I wiped the counter down where it didn't really need wiping just so I could look busy and focus on something else. 'I've been busy. Focusing on the business.' I winced inwardly. *That was a very Belinda thing to say.*

'It seems pretty quiet today,' he said.

He was right. Not a table was occupied.

'It is,' I snapped, which shocked me;

176

I'm not really a snappy person. 'But it's not always like this.' I wiped the counter again, more vigorously. 'Hence the fact I've been busy.'

'Okay. I believe you. I haven't seen you in the pub for ages.'

'I haven't *been* in the pub for ages.' There was a beat, then I had to say something. 'I just didn't want to be there and have to witness you playing happy families with . . . *her*. Not after what happened at Christmas. Remember, I had a boyfriend who made our relationship extremely complicated. It's not something I'm willing to go through again. You two are together. End of.'

'She told me she was pregnant. What else could I do? It was my child — I had to agree to try again.'

'Last time I saw her, she didn't look very pregnant.' I realised that I may have sounded a little snipey there, but it was true.

'Yeah.' He shrugged, then flushed and looked pained and uncomfortable. 'That's because she's not.'

'She's not *now*? Or she wasn't ever?' I knew the answer of course, but some nasty little part of me wanted to twist the knife. Why the hell had he been taken in by her for so long? And what tale had she spun him in the end?

'It was a false alarm. But she said she really wanted a baby; begged me to keep it all quiet while we worked through it.'

Lies, lies, lies.

I opened my mouth to say something to that effect, but then snapped it shut. This was their business, and I didn't want to be the one to drive a wedge between them. He had to be the one to see sense and do the right thing.

'She was really cut up about it.'

And the Oscar goes to . . . I wanted to say.

Instead, I said, 'Why is any of this relevant to me?'

'I wanted to be the one to tell you.'

'It really makes no difference to me, Sam. It's your life. Your relationship. You have to decide how to move forwards with it. Whether you want to try again.' The words almost choked me. 'Or whether you cut your losses. All I know is if things weren't great between me and my partner, the last thing I'd want is to bring a baby into the mix. It's a recipe for disaster.'

'Well, all *I* know is that she needs me at the minute — and you're right, Cerys, we need to sort things out before we try again.'

But if there had *been a baby, are you absolutely sure it was even yours?* I wanted to say. But, of course, again, I didn't. I clamped my mouth shut and went back to my counter cleaning.

'I need to get on, Sam. I'm sorry about the situation. But it's nothing to do with me. I am truly sorry.'

'You always apologise,' he said softly. 'And it's never your fault.'

'Maybe not. But this is an impossible position for me, and I don't think we can do anything about it.' I paused in my cleaning and looked up at him. I was horrified to realise his eyes were all swimmy, and that meant that I was only seconds away from ugly crying everywhere myself. I had to get him out of the shop before that happened. 'You need to work through this. You know where I am, but I'm not going to hold onto a Christmas kiss forever. Goodbye, Sam.'

And I turned away without letting him respond and began fiddling with the coffee machine.

It was a few moments later that I heard his footsteps retreat and the bell go above the door, signalling that he'd left my shop.

And then I did cry for a little bit. Honestly, Belinda was *such* a nasty piece of work, and you could be absolutely certain that she would act the tragic girl-friend a little bit longer, just until she thought it was the right time to abandon Sam again and leave even more chaos in her wake.

There had to be something I could do — but I didn't quite know when the opportunity would present itself.

Until, that is, my brother turned up

that day in December, and then it all became clear . . .

★ ★ ★

So, if you've been following this story, and I hope you have been, you might understand now why my Dickensian-themed shepherding stunt resulted in such an awkward moment, when I was forced to speak at length to Sam.

Still smelling faintly of wet wool, I took the drinks back to our table, my face burning and my stomach somersaulting. It was *such* an awkward moment because Belinda was still there. She'd hung around like a bad smell all through the summer, but I knew she was just biding her time until she could get the tenants out. I found myself eavesdropping more and more on her conversations in the tea room. None of them were as indiscreet as the first one I'd heard, and she was clever enough to talk to her friends in more hushed tones from the table in the corner she favoured — right next to an electricity socket for her laptop, I hasten to add. But it was one of those situations where, because I knew the background, I was filling in the blanks. I knew that she wanted to spend more time in London, and she was trying to work out how she could do it.

One conversation, for example, went something like this:

'Yeah, well, it's just the same really. I said I needed more time to think about it, and I didn't know if I wanted to do it again right away because I was still trying to get over the disappointment blah blah blah . . . but the more I *do* think about it, the more I think I really don't want to do it. But because I'm kind of stuck until I get the tenants out, I don't have a choice. It's *incredibly* frustrating. They've got a twelve-month lease. Not sure how much longer I can put him off, you know? I actually think I need to go and see . . . someone . . . and get something . . . to stop it happening?'

I instinctively knew she was talking about trying for a baby, but anyone else overhearing her might think she was just talking about work.

She was clever. Very clever. I had to give her that.

I really wanted to go to Sam and tell him. But she'd deny it was about anything other than work. And who was he most likely to believe? His girlfriend, or me, the girl he'd kissed once at Christmas when we were both as confused as each other and swept up in all the magic?

But, you know, sometimes when you think there'll never be a way out, something presents itself to you. And that something takes root and grows, and then suddenly you can see what you can do to make things better.

To be honest, I would have suffered in silence as long as it took, had this one thing not happened at the Spatchcock in the run-up to Christmas.

So, on the night of the marauding sheep, I put the drinks on the table and heaved myself back into my chair. I could feel by the tension in my face that I was scowling.

'Are you okay?' Edie asked. 'Sheep situation too much for you?'

'It's probably me,' said Geraint. He'd calmed down a bit now, probably after being quizzed — and no doubt mocked a little, if I'm honest — by my friend. 'I shouldn't have come.'

I sighed. 'Oh, you should have. You're bloody annoying, boy, but you're my big brother so you're *allowed* to be annoying.'

'Thanks, sis. I think it'll just take a while to really get her out of my system, you know?'

'Probably best to have a few more one-night stands,' said Edie, nodding in what she probably thought was a wise fashion. 'Truly get over the bitch. You know?' She sipped her drink thoughtfully, and I fought back the urge to tell her to follow her own advice to get over Ninian Chambers.

'One was enough.' Geraint shuddered. 'She was completely full-on. Before I knew it, I was rather merry and in her house, and . . . well, we were ill-prepared and not very careful, as far as I recall.'

He blushed a bit, and I pulled a face. *TMI, brother dear.*

'Geraint, I hope you're not telling me that you could potentially be riddled with an unspeakable disease because you were careless with your one-night stand?'

'No! I honestly don't have anything. But I mean, we hadn't even exchanged numbers — so even if I'd wanted to get back in touch with her, I couldn't. It was totally meaningless on both sides.'

'Oh God, it gets worse,' I muttered. 'You're bonkers. Absolutely bonkers.'

'Or bonking,' added Edie helpfully.

'Edie!' I glared at her and she shrugged her shoulders. Then she looked past me and her lip curled into a sort of terrifying scowl. 'It's her. It's that Woman.'

I didn't want to look. I knew from the amount of vitriol in her comment that the only 'Woman' Edie was talking about was Sam's 'Woman'. Belinda.

'Why the hell didn't she stay in London? And why the hell doesn't she go back there?' grumbled Edie. 'The woman gives me bad vibes.'

'Rented out the mews house, apparently,' I said. 'On a twelve-month lease. Give her time.'

'Mews house?' Geraint popped his head up like one of those bash-a-mole games. 'The girl I met last year, she had a mews house. Very swish.'

'Must be a type then,' said Edie.

But then I couldn't hear anything else for the buzzing in my ears and the *kerchunk*, *kerching* of pennies dropping and pieces fitting together . . .

It couldn't be.

Could it?

'Geraint,' I said slowly. 'Try not to react, but turn around and have a look at the woman who's just walked into the bar, will you?'

'Sure.' My brother looked puzzled, but obediently he turned around.

And that was it.

I saw his shoulders stiffen and his knuckles clench, as he did the very opposite to 'don't react'. He reacted in the maddest way possible.

'It's you!' he yelled and jumped out of his seat. 'Oh my *God*!'

Belinda's head shot around, and her face flickered through a few expressions, including disbelief, horror and deep, deep embarrassment.

However, it remained a fact that this woman was a pro at lies and deceit — and obviously at cheating on her boyfriend as well — so it only took a split second for her face to rearrange itself into disgust and revulsion.

'I don't know what you're talking about,' she hissed, glaring at him. 'I've absolutely no idea who you are.'

'London. Last year. Apples and Pears? Brick Lane? Open mic? Cocktails . . . ? Yeah?'

'Who the *hell* are you?' She gave him one last withering look and stalked off.

I would have loved, absolutely *loved*, for him to go 'you're the woman I had a liaison with at Christmas, when we were both rather merry and ill-prepared . . .'

But, of course, he didn't oblige me by

saying that out loud so all and sundry could listen.

Instead, he turned to me, his face white and pinched: 'She's the woman I had a liaison with at Christmas, when we were both rather merry and ill-prepared . . . the mews house woman. Oh bloody *hell*.'

Oh bloody hell indeed.

11

Christmas Present

I bundled Geraint out of there as soon as I could. He downed his whisky, and we hurried away before he let anything else slip. I *knew* my brother; if he thought he was right, then he'd hang on and stand his ground as long as he possibly could — I guess that was exactly what he was doing with the Alwen situation.

We picked over it all again at my flat, once I'd had a chance to take the costume off and get into my own very delightful, very modern and very soft leggings and sweater, although Edie did comment that I should have kept the make-up on a bit longer as it gave my face 'character'. Anyway, it seemed Geraint was certain that Belinda was the woman from his one-night stand.

The whole thing kept me awake again that night, as I went over and over it all in my head. Belinda had been the one Geraint had slept with. There could have been a very real possibility that she'd suspected she was pregnant after that, but rather than take the chance, she'd come back to Sam, perhaps intending to use him as a cover story for the pregnancy — who knew? But then it had turned out to be a false alarm and she'd messed up the chance of getting back to London quickly by sticking tenants in the mews house for a year, and in doing so she'd backed herself into a corner.

I mean, there was the chance she'd go back to London pretty soon if the yearly lease was coming up. But what if she tried to get Sam to leave as well? I knew it was unlikely, but nothing was impossible. I guess it boiled down to how much he wanted to make it work with her and how much more he was prepared to give.

Poor Sam. He was far too Lovely to have his life dictated by what Belinda wanted, because that's what it was beginning to seem like to me.

I recalled all the conversations she'd

had in my tea room and a plan began to form.

I crept through the flat and rummaged in my brother's bag, took out something that I hoped would be very useful, and padded back to bed.

The plan I was pondering would mean taking a big chance. But it was worth it.

* * *

I didn't have much chance to do anything about the plan the next day, because that morning I waved goodbye to a rather subdued Geraint and started with some other, rather last-minute, planning for the Christmas Craft Fair. It had definitely become a bit of a Christmas tradition, and it was due to be held tonight.

Unfortunately, it was now raining and the light flurries of snow from the previous evening had gone; it just didn't look as Christmassy as it might have done. The rain had eased up by lunchtime though, and Edie and I were all hands on deck getting the tables out and the seats arranged. Then we stopped for a hot chocolate and a gingerbread man and a moan about the weather.

'It might have been nice if it had snowed properly this year,' Edie said, then pursed her lips and sucked the cream off the top of her hot chocolate thoughtfully.

'It would have been lovely. I think the street would have looked gorgeous. I mean, I know we've got the tree and the fairy lights, and the shop windows are done, but the problem would then have been whether people could make it or not?' I fished a marshmallow out of the depths of my own mug before it dissolved completely. 'Nobody likes driving in the snow, and it would have stopped people getting here from the other villages.'

'I like driving in the snow.' I jumped as Sam's voice broke into my thoughts, whispering into my ear, and I felt his warm breath on my neck. *Where had he sprung from?* I flushed as red as Rudolph's nose. I'd done so well avoiding him, yet here he was, right next to me. And now I knew the information about Belinda and my brother, it made me even more intensely uncomfortable with the whole situation.

But he was very close to me, and despite everything that's all I could seem to focus on . . .

'You only like it because you've got a big all-terrain thing,' replied Edie, nonplussed. 'Normal people with normal cars don't like it.' The woman had ears like a bat, I swear.

'What she said,' I replied, nodding towards my friend even as my heart bounded around in my chest like a toddler on a selection box sugar-high. 'We need people to visit us.'

'I suppose so.' Sam stood up and looked at the tables. 'Who am I sharing with this year? You again, I hope?'

'Oh God, Sam, I'm so sorry — but you're not sharing with anyone. Let alone me.' I felt myself flush again. When he'd emailed in response to my very generic blanket email to confirm he wanted a table, I determined there and then to give him his own, well away from ours. I didn't think my heart could take his proximity this year, especially not now, not after knowing what I knew. If my tongue was loosened by his so-called moonshine, I might say something we would all live to regret. And seeing him here, and finding myself just as attracted to him as I'd always been, I knew deep inside it was just safer that way.

I broke the news to him. 'You're over by the carollers — next to the mulled wine lady. I think you'll do well there, because people will feel merry and want to buy alcohol when people are singing carols nearby and their inhibitions are lowered.'

'Oh. Okay — well, yes. I see the logic in that,' said Sam, but he did look a little dejected and I felt awful. Why couldn't I accept his friendship and just move on, grateful for the fact I still had him in my life? 'People could well be merry, couldn't they?'

'Merry.' Edie nodded in agreement. 'Or the alcohol will be extraordinarily kind to people, and dull their senses enough so they don't have to hear the carollers belting out the wrong notes. Actually, speaking of music, Cerys, couldn't you—'

'No! No way!' I yelped, looking at her in horror, knowing her too well and realising what she was thinking. 'I did very well to sing last Christmas at the pub. I don't intend to start doing mock-festivals in the middle of the street.'

'A few songs around the Padcock Christmas Tree isn't a festival,' said Edie, far too reasonably.

I shook my head. 'Look, I'm not saying I didn't enjoy last year—' then I wanted to curl up and hide somewhere, because I remembered *exactly* how much I enjoyed last year, especially That Kiss on the towpath '—but that's a little different.'

'I really hope you'll sing again at the pub this year, Cerys. Last Christmas Eve was amazing,' said Sam. He sounded so

genuine my heart broke a little. I wondered if he just meant the singing, or
what happened afterwards, and I shook
my head again, not wanting to overthink
or get upset.

'Maybe,' I said.

'Tell you what,' said Sam, 'shall we
make a bargain?'

Despite my resolve, I looked directly
at him, a little confused. 'A bargain?'

'Yes. If it snows for your Craft Fair,
will you sing at the pub on Christmas
Eve again?'

I chanced a glance at the sky. It still
looked wet and not at all snowy. That was
good. But not good enough. 'Hold on.'
I dug my phone out of my pocket, and
Googled 'today's weather in Padcock'.
Google told me the rain would clear, it
would be dry all day and the temper-
ature well above freezing. I was safe. I
puffed out a breath. 'Okay. If it snows
tonight at the Craft Fair, I'll play at the
Spatchcock on Christmas Eve.'

'Brilliant.' Sam grinned. 'Do you
promise?'

I nodded. 'I . . . promise?'

'Good. I'll see you later then.' He raised his hand in a wave and walked off cheerfully.

After that, Edie and I finished our hot chocolate and got everything sorted, and then we went back inside the tea room to start getting our own produce ready.

About an hour before the fair was due to open, I was carrying a tray of freshly made rum truffles, shaped like Christmas puddings, over to the front door, when I heard a piece of heavy machinery pulling up outside.

'What on earth? The roads are meant to be closed to traffic tonight!' I looked at Edie in a panic, and she looked at me, and we raced to the door to see what was going on.

And right there, right outside my tea room, we stepped into a blizzard of snow.

'What the flippity-flip is going on?' Edie stared at me, her jaw hanging open most unattractively.

'I have *no* idea.' I walked a bit further into the street and saw a massive black thing spouting fake snow out of a tube and into the air. The fake snow was falling down and covering the Craft Fair area.

I mean, it looked stunning, but then my heart began to pound. And I knew — I knew in an instant what had happened.

And sure enough, Sam stepped out from behind the massive machine and gave whoever was operating it a thumbs up sign. Then he walked through the blizzard so we were soon standing face to face. His hands were in his pockets and fake snowflakes were in his hair, and his eyes were warm and his smile was warmer.

'Cerys, will you play in the pub again on Christmas Eve, please? Look — it's snowing on your Craft Fair, and a promise is a promise.'

'It is — but how? I mean — *how*?' I gestured to the snow machine and then waved my arms in the air, indicating the blizzard all around us. 'I mean I know — *how*. But . . . how?'

'Some of the *Christmas Carol* special

effects guys were staying at the pub last night — the machinery was parked up nearby.' He shrugged. 'Let's just say I don't have much home-brew or gin left to sell tonight. But it was worth it. Or, at least, it *will* be worth it, come Christmas Eve. If you play for us again.'

'I can't really say no. Or can I?' I stared at him, unable to tear my gaze away from his.

'No,' he said, smiling gently. 'You can't.'

And, to be honest, I didn't want to.

★ ★ ★

The Christmas Craft Fair was more of a success than ever. The 'snow' made it even more special, and the carollers looked fantastic, all bundled up and jolly and singing loudly by the tree. I didn't see much of Sam — he really didn't have much left to sell, and his stall soon closed down. I'm sure he'd closed it down with a smile and a promise that he'd restock and have it all available at the Spatchcock just as soon as he could.

At one point though, I looked up and Belinda was there talking to him. And then I looked again . . . and they'd both gone.

★ ★ ★

The snowy Craft Fair was the most popular discussion topic in the village for a couple of weeks. But I was kind of distracted, because the more time marched on, and the closer Christmas became, the more I thought about the way Belinda was treating Sam — and I couldn't bear to think about someone so lovely being used like that.

Finally, on the twenty-first of December, after Edie had spent an hour complaining that she still hadn't wrapped her presents and then mindlessly eaten every last chocolate in our tea room advent calendar, I told her to take the rest of the day off. She looked horrified when I announced it.

'Why don't you want the day off?' I asked. 'You said you had presents to wrap. You're clearly distracted and, to be fair, not very useful today. Plus, you've eaten all the advent calendar chocolates and tomorrow was *my* day to have the chocolate.'

'Really? Gosh — they never last until Christmas Eve, do they? Well, I do still have presents to wrap. But I don't buy for many people, and what else am I supposed to do after I've wrapped them?' She genuinely didn't seem to think she had anything else to do.

'I don't know. Draw. Paint. Get your mojo back. Work on your freelancing. Cyber-stalk Ninian Chambers.'

Her eyes flashed at his name. 'I think,' she said stiffly, 'I shall wrap my presents and go and work on my computer.' She started heading out of the door, looking quite peeved and put out. 'And I mean work. I will not be looking up Ninian Chambers.'

I knew for a fact that meant she'd be doing some cyber-stalking of the said

Ninian Chambers. I'd even found some Google searches on our work laptop in the history. One day I'd get to the bottom of her obsession with him. I would indeed.

When Edie had gone, I waited in the tea room, part of me praying that Belinda would swan in. I hadn't seen her here since my brother had turned up at the pub, and I suspected that she might have been staying away because she'd seen Geraint with us — but I also knew that she was so utterly brazen she'd probably just continue to deny it and, again, we would be back to 'who would Sam believe?'

Plus, the tea room was the only place in the village that had free WiFi, and I knew that eventually her desire to get out of the flat above the pub and into her virtual London life would outweigh any qualms she may have had whilst she was considering where to go. Honestly, pre-Geraint I had felt like charging her rent. I'd even considered changing the WiFi password so she'd have to come and ask me for it, which would gall her, or perhaps I'd disconnect that socket she liked to use . . . although I'd probably just have to stick duct tape over it because, let's face it, I had no idea how to disconnect a socket. Then I could sit and watch her try and pick it off with her perfect nails . . .

I was just standing there thinking those thoughts and wishing she'd appear, uncomfortable that she'd fallen off my radar and could be telling all sorts of lies, when the bell above the door tinkled.

I looked up, and, like Beelzebub himself, there she was in the doorway, glowering and peering into the corner to ensure 'her' table was free.

Dammit! I could have just piled dirty crockery on it, and then watched her struggle with the lead of the laptop to make it stretch. That was something to bear in mind for the future, but right now I had to focus on the fact that Awful Belinda was *In. My. Tea. Room.*

Okay, I had *wanted* her to come in, but now she was actually here I felt a little sick — because today might, just *might*, be my chance to put my plan into action.

I watched the cowbag plug her laptop in and arrange all her office stuff around her. I wondered if she genuinely missed working out of the London cafés, or it really was because she couldn't bear to be in the flat any longer than she had to be. She'd brought this on herself at the end of the day though, and I couldn't feel sorry for her.

I watched her carefully until she'd logged on and started tapping away at the keyboard, then took my chance and, slipping quietly past her, I turned the sign to 'closed' to stop anyone else coming in and disrupting things. Then I took my position up at the counter whilst she barked her orders across at me. Today it was a black coffee with skimmed milk on the side.

Pretty soon she picked up her phone, cast a quick glance at me and stood up.

My stomach somersaulted. I knew with a horrible certainty that today was going to be the day, and I knew I had to be quick.

Belinda started walking towards the loos, and, once she was past the counter, I turned, picked up my phone and ran through the kitchen out into the back yard. I stopped at the toilet window. Thankfully, I'd had the foresight to leave it wide open . . . and sure enough, I heard her voice from within the building. 'Jools! Oh my God, thank *God* you're back from holiday. I had to call you. I had to get out of there and call you just as soon as I could — guess what? Just guess who I bumped into a couple of weeks ago? Or guess who I pretended I didn't *know* a couple of weeks ago . . .' I couldn't stop myself from making a face when she laughed a deep, throaty, sexy laugh. 'No, not him. I wish! I've always had a thing for men in uniform, you *know* that. No. It was the guy from Apples and Pears. Yes! Him! No idea what he was doing here, but he shouted across the pub to me. My God, I had a lucky escape there. I just acted like he was crazy. I couldn't wake up to that pained expression every morning, I'll give you that for free! Honestly, if he hadn't backed out apologising, I might even have pretended I was asleep, just so he could have crept out and I wouldn't have to look at him any more.'

I stiffened. That was my brother she was talking about! My big brother, who, yes, I had to acknowledge, did have rather a pained expression on his face most of the time due to the fact that he was yearning for his lost love . . . or thinking about the next piece of music he had to play. But there was no need for her to be so mean. Geraint had a lot of redeeming features, he really did.

Belinda continued talking, her words tumbling out excitedly. It seemed there was no stopping her and she'd been bottling all this up for ages. 'Anyway, I just had to tell you. Oh — I got everything sorted as well, so if it happens again I'll be safe. I don't want to go through that again. I've decided I really don't want kids any time soon. I'm going to have to tell Sam at some point — I just need to pick my time. He's probably already choosing nursery décor, and I saw him looking up family houses to buy on the Internet the other day, and it's absolutely *not* what I want. Not with him and not here, and he'll never move away from this bloody place. I can't bear the thought of being stuck here with kids. I'd need to be somewhere with a bit more going on. I absolutely cannot *wait* to come home. I'm literally counting the weeks until I get those people out . . .'

I'd heard enough. I looked down at my hand, almost forgetting I had my own phone in it. I wandered back to the tea room, heard the Christmas music playing gently in the background, but, almost like an automaton, I switched it off, followed by the coffee machine and the fridges and the fairy lights I had draped around the place. All of a sudden the café was silent and darker; no comforting hum of machinery or gentle buzzing of the lights, no sound of the coffee machine doing its odd little splurts and splutters (*no idea why my coffee machine does that. It has a mind of its own*), no mellow soundtrack in the background.

When Belinda eventually came out of the toilets, she stood there in the semi-darkness, staring around her and then looked across at me, clearly confused.

I locked eyes with her for a moment, then switched everything back on.

'Sorry. Thought it was a power cut. But it was a false alarm.' I held her gaze a moment longer. 'As you were.' I smiled politely, nodding back to her laptop. She could interpret *that* any way she wanted it.

She didn't smile back, but she flushed; it had been enough, I think, to unsettle her. She walked back to the seat, hid her phone away, drank her coffee and concentrated on her laptop.

She didn't stay long after that.

As she was packing up her stuff to leave, I went over to retrieve the empty cup and untouched milk (the little jug was still full — *such a waste*) and fixed her with a look as hard as granite . . . I hoped. That was the 'look' I was aiming for, anyway.

'My brother sends his regards,' I said. 'He had to dash away early, but I'm sure that's not the first time he's done that to you.'

Then I picked up the crockery and went back over to the counter.

I listened for the ding of the bell over the door.

It came pretty quickly.

12

Christmas Present

I had to be quick for the next stage of my plan. It was coming up to lunchtime, and I didn't want her to have too much time back at the flat. It was possible she could pack and go in the few hours we had until the pub got really busy in the evening. But the Spatchcock was open, and quite popular for lunch, so that was good enough for me.

I hurried down the street and into the pub, and my heart did that little jolt, as it always did, when I saw Sam there, laughing at something one of the older men from the village had said. Sam had time for everyone. He never minded if they told him the same stories over and over. He acted as if he was interested in them every time the information was shared.

It was one of the many things I realised I loved about him, and my stomach turned over. He didn't deserve the way Belinda was treating him. Not at all.

I took a deep breath and marched over to the bar. Sam looked my way and his face lit up.

He came over to me and smiled into my eyes. 'Cerys. It's so good to see you. The Craft Fair was amazing yet again. I can't believe it was a couple of weeks ago — it's been absolutely crazy at the pub and I bet you've been the same. I have to say, I didn't have much to take home with me from the Fair, but I'm on it. Look — restocked shelves.' He indicated the shelves behind the bar that were now filled with his colourful, artisan-looking gin bottles.

I screwed up my nose and shook my head. 'You had nothing to take home with you, and we both know this, because you bribed a snow machine man. And *that* was even more amazing than the fair. Thank you. But honestly Sam, I'm here to see Belinda.'

'You're more than welcome. But . . . what? *Belinda*?' He had a good right to look surprised. When had I ever voluntarily put myself in the way of that cow?

'Seriously, I am. But do me a favour. Tell her that it's someone asking about her scarves. She won't come down if she knows it's me.'

'Well, I think she's in the snug actually,' he said. 'She went in there with her laptop. You can go in to see her? Might be easier?'

'Great. Yes. Yes, I will. Thank you, Sam.'

And, squaring my shoulders, I marched in.

Belinda was sitting in the corner, tapping furiously away on her laptop. She must have linked into the WiFi in the flat in order to continue to build her empire.

I took a deep breath and walked over to her. 'Hello, Belinda.'

'Go away.' She didn't even bother to look up. 'I'm busy.'

'What? Busy sending private messages to your mates about the situation you've put Sam in?'

Her fingers faltered, but she still didn't

look up.

I pressed my point home a little. 'It's a shame, from your point of view, that you didn't do that earlier, instead of having all those weird phone calls in my tea room.'

She just snorted a sour little laugh. 'Weird phone calls? Darling, you're just spouting rubbish.'

'No, I'm really not.'

'Yes. You really are. I don't know what you think I've been saying, but I think you're mistaken. Really I do.'

'Hmm.' I paused. My heart was hammering now. I had one chance at this. I prayed I wouldn't blow it. 'I'd not be too sure about that. Now, are you going to tell Sam what's been going on, or shall I?'

She slammed her laptop lid down and glared at me. I think she might have tried to flounce out, but I had her cornered. My Border collie training had come in useful again — who would have thought it? I just had to fight the urge to drop to my knees and growl menacingly.

It had always worked with Geraint, but he wasn't quite as judgemental as I felt Belinda might be. He just used to snarl back to make a point, but then he knew who the boss was.

'I have no need to tell Sam anything. Who the hell do you think he'll believe anyway, even if you go to him with made-up crap? His girlfriend, or the girl who works in the craft shop?'

'I own the craft shop, actually. On a very basic level, we are both business-women. However, I have a premises, whereas you seem to work out of cor-ners wherever you can grab free WiFi.' I paused again to silently congratulate myself on that one. Then I resumed. 'I have not rented my premises out for twelve months while I decided if I was pregnant or not with a man I had a one-night stand with. I haven't lied to my partner. I haven't continued to lie — All. This. Time.' I leaned my hands on the table and brought my face quite close to hers. 'I am not keeping my partner hanging on so I've got bed and board while he thinks I'm just not ready to try for another baby. I'm not waiting for my tenants to get out so I can bugger off again and leave even more upset in my wake. Now. I can make this easy for you, or I can make it hard for you.'

'You can do nothing of the sort. Again. Where's your proof? You're the only one who thinks she's heard these things. So, you've not got a leg to stand on — whatever lies you try to tell him. Again, who will he believe?' She looked triumphant for a moment, but I did detect a little flicker of alarm in her eyes. *Good.*

'I don't need anything to back me up, or show proof, except a little bit of technology.' I laid my phone on the table in front of her and pressed a button. 'Just have a listen to that. Now, who do you think that is?'

She glared at me and picked it up as if it would burn her, her eyes never leaving my face.

Her face, on the other hand, paled when she heard what I'd recorded that morning on the voice recorder app:

'My God, I had a lucky escape there. I just acted like he was crazy. I couldn't wake up to that pained expression every morning, I'll give you that for free! Honestly, if he hadn't backed out apologising, I might even have pretended I was asleep, just so he could have crept out and I wouldn't have to look at him any more.'

'You bitch!' she hissed. 'How dare you?'

'And how dare you screw around with my brother when you're supposed to be in a relationship with one of my friends? Bitch yourself!' I realised that possibly sounded a little 'playground', but I was seething.

Then her face went stony and she glared at me. 'Well, all of this is pretty easily resolved,' she said. Quick as a flash, she deleted the recording and handed me the phone back. 'Good luck with spreading lies about me, darling.'

'Ah-ha.' I nodded, trying not to throw up. I had a back-up plan, and I prayed now that it would succeed. Because if it didn't, I was definitely the one who was screwed.

Diving into my bag, I pulled out a CD. It was one of those blank ones you could copy music onto, and I'd written two words on the front: *Belinda's Confession*.

I held it up, out of her reach, even as she made a grab for it. 'Oh *darling*,' I said, 'you don't think I'm that naïve, do you? I have it all, right here. Plus a couple more back-ups, just in case. It doesn't take long to transfer stuff onto a computer and burn it on a CD. I've even got this morning's little conversation, so it really doesn't matter that you've accidentally deleted that there. Now, in a few seconds, I'm going to call Sam in and hand this over to him. You've got all of that time to decide what to do.' I held her gaze for a moment. 'You can, of course, bow out gracefully. Make something up and walk away with your head held high. If you do, you have my word that I won't say anything to him. It's entirely up to you. But I do think you need to make a decision pretty quickly.' I turned and walked over to the bar. My hand was hovering over the little bell that would summon Sam to the snug bar.

Then I took a deep breath and hit it.

13

Christmas Present

Sure enough, Sam came through the little door and smiled when he saw me. 'Hey, Cerys. Can I help?'

'Err, yeah.' I held the CD up, being careful to obscure the writing on it with my fingers. 'New music you can put on, right now. I just wanted to—'

'*Sam!*'

In Welsh folklore, there's a creature called the *Gwrach-y-Rhibyn*. She's a hag-like woman who wails and screeches, a veritable portent of doom. She travels alongside people, then suddenly shrieks in their ear. One of her cries is '*Fy ngŵr, fy ngŵr!*'. Which basically translates into, 'My husband! My husband!'

I think I would have been forgiven by anyone in that moment for believing the *Gwrach-y-Rhibyn* had appeared by my right-hand side and wailed in my ear, so shrill and panicked was Belinda's voice — although, I suppose Sam wasn't technically her husband.

'Oh! Wow. Belinda.' He looked a bit startled, and even more so when she practically pushed me out of the way and started to snottily cry. I wasn't sure how much of it was put on, but I was willing to bet a lot of it was anger and a good proportion of what was left simply frustration she'd been caught out.

'I need to speak to you, Sam. Now. Right now. It won't wait.'

'Okay.' His face paled and he looked at me. 'But Cerys—'

'Forget bloody Cerys!' cried Belinda. This time she did shove me, and I wobbled.

'Cerys!' Sam held his hand out as if he could stop me from falling, but I just shook my head and moved back voluntarily.

'It's okay. Talk to Belinda.'

'Is that for me, though?' He pointed to the CD.

'No. It's fine. Not yet. You need to

speak to her first,' I said and stepped away from the bar. But I decided to leave things on an ominous note, so she knew I meant business. 'Let me know what happens, and I can give you this in a little while if need be.'

Sam looked confused, as he had a good right to be, but Belinda just looked mortified and wailed again, shaking her head.

I felt this was a good time to slip into the shadows.

So, I slipped into them and let Sam and Belinda disappear into the flat, up the little staircase marked 'Private'. I sidled out of the snug into the main bar and dipped under the counter so I could find the honesty box.

Sometimes Sam was the only person serving, and if he had to leave the bar for any reason he put out his honesty box. The people of Padcock were very honest and all knew where to get their favourite tipples from, so it worked well. I put the box on the counter, found his laminated note that apologised for not being there, left the hinged portion of the counter open in case anyone needed to get a gin or a real ale or anything, and then I left.

I left the Spatchcock and walked and walked, down the canal towpath as far as the next village, and then back again.

Part of me felt mean and ghastly for doing what I'd just done. But the larger part of me was pleased I'd done it.

And, with any luck, the demo CD of Welsh folk songs I'd pilfered from my brother's bag could just stay out of the equation all together.

★　★　★

I wasn't really surprised to hear a knock on my door that evening. Taking a deep breath, I opened it and saw Edie standing there, her eyes wide and wild and her boots planted firmly on my doorstep.

'The Bitch has left,' she announced. 'A taxi came for her earlier! I watched as she loaded all her stuff back into it. He came and threw some stuff in as well. I wasn't close enough to hear, but Veronica swears she heard him say 'please don't bother coming back this time'. Then he just walked away without a backward glance.'

'Backtrack a bit, please. The Bitch?' I looked at Edie a little blankly. Edie had nicknames for many, many people and also disliked many, many people, so I wasn't entirely sure who she meant, but I had a good idea and hoped she didn't notice me crossing my fingers behind my back.

'Yeah.' She indicated that she wanted to come in, so I stepped aside and let her into my hallway. 'Awful Belinda.' She turned to me and smiled. 'She's been promoted to The Bitch. No idea what happened with those two, but I will make it my mission to find out.'

I shook my head and folded my arms. 'No need to. *I* happened.'

'What?' Edie blinked and stared at me. 'Did Sam see sense? Oh my *God*!' She grabbed my hands in hers and practically jumped up and down. 'Did he bin her off?'

I half-smiled, but inside I felt a bit wretched. It struck me that I *had* done this. I'd probably, indirectly, broken Sam's heart.

'I'm not sure. I just didn't like the way Belinda was treating him. I told her a few home truths this morning. She'd dragged my brother into it, and that was unacceptable.'

Edie looked at me for a few more moments; long enough to make me feel uncomfortable. 'I see,' was all she said eventually. 'She's definitely gone. The pub is closed tonight. Not even the honesty box is up. It is literally, actually, closed.'

'Wow.'

'Yeah. And it's what, three days until Christmas? Do you think he'll open up for Christmas Eve?'

I shrugged and gently released my hands. 'I have no idea, Edie. I have no idea.'

And I didn't.

14

Christmas Present

As you can imagine, the closure of the Spatchcock was big news in Padcock; even bigger news than the fake snow at the Christmas Craft Fair. None of the villagers could really get past the fact that, just a few weeks ago, we'd all been in there celebrating the end of filming *A Christmas Carol*, before being stampeded by sheep . . . and now, dark windows and not a whisper of Christmas music. The rumours were rife.

It had spread like wildfire that Belinda had left, but obviously, without all the facts, people were making things up and tongues were wagging.

'I heard,' said Veronica to her friends as they all sat in my tea room, 'that she picked up with a rock star in London and that's why she went.'

'Well, I heard she'd had an offer from

Harrods to set up a franchise in the store,' said Mrs Culpepper. 'And Sam's a local boy. He wouldn't want to uproot himself. She had to make the choice and Harrods won.'

'Cerys, love, you're close to Sam,' said Veronica. 'Do you know what happened with him and Belinda?'

'I don't think I'm any closer to him than anyone else in the village,' I said, forcing a smile. 'Your guess is as good as mine.'

'But you two always seem such good friends. He's always smiling when you're around. He never smiled so much when *she* was around, mind you . . .' Then Veronica looked at me a little appraisingly as she no doubt put two and two together and came up with fifty-five.

'Will that be all, ladies?' I asked, trying to retain my professionalism as I put their cakes and coffees down.

'For now,' said Mrs Culpepper darkly. 'For now.'

★ ★ ★

I couldn't wait to close up shop on Christmas Eve. The queries hadn't stopped, and Sam still hadn't reappeared. Luckily, Jay, the part-time barman, had saved the day and opened the Spatchcock up the day before Christmas Eve. Everyone was happy to see the local open again, but still the curiosity and rumours were rumbling around the village.

It was a small place, and these things happened. But one thing was clear — not one person had a good word to say for Belinda. Whatever had occurred, everyone seemed to automatically assume she was the one at fault.

I knew, of course, that this was definitely the case — Belinda was *so* the one at fault — but I'd promised her I wouldn't stir things up if she left. I was thinking about this, amongst other things, as I locked up and then retraced my steps down to the canal towpath.

I couldn't help but think of this time last year, late on Christmas Eve, when Sam and I had been wandering down here and one thing had led to another.

At least this year I was actually aware I'd be performing that evening — the Snow Machine Night had trapped me into that one — and, regardless of whatever had happened between Sam, Belinda and myself, I didn't want to let Sam and the villagers down. In fact, I had a play-list organised, and my black dress was already hanging up to get the creases out of it. Jay had said he would sort the stool out for me and I hoped, I really hoped, that Sam would turn up to see at least part of my performance. I'd suddenly realised I was doing it as much for me as I was for him, and I wanted to be able to thank him afterwards for making me see the joy in performing again.

I was spending the next day, Christmas Day, with Edie, and she'd already told me the timings of 'White Christmas' and *Willy Wonka* on television so we could plan lunch around them, and my parents and brother were coming down to me for New Year. Geraint had said he'd do a duet with me in a special one-off show at the Spatchcock, although we'd unanimously agreed to not do the 'dead pigeon' song, which was probably for the best.

My heart lifted a little and I smiled to myself. But still it remained that there was only one more thing to do — one more person I needed to see today.

Although it was only about four o'clock, it was getting quite dark. Up ahead, I could see the lamp post we'd stood under the previous year . . . and there was a figure leaning against it. The figure looked terribly familiar, even though he was bundled up against the cold with his coat collar up, a scarf around his neck and his hands buried deep into his pockets.

I hesitated. Now I was here I didn't know if I wanted to walk towards him, or to run as fast as I could towards him. But my decision was made for me when his head snapped up and he turned to look straight at me. He pushed himself away from the lamp post and faced me but didn't take any steps. It was as if he was frozen in time, just standing there, waiting for something.

Waiting for me?

I walked. I closed the gap as if I'd lost all power of reason. I knew, deep down, we needed to have this conversation.

'Hey.' His voice sounded tired as I approached until I was standing in front of him, but it also sounded warm.

'Hey. Fancy meeting you here.' It was a bit flippant, but I didn't really know how else to react.

'I just thought I'd come for a walk. Have a think. See who I bumped into.'

'Well. Here I am.' I shrugged. 'Sorry if you would have preferred someone else to bump into.'

'No. You're the best person I could have possibly bumped into.' He looked up at the sky and frowned. 'I think it's going to snow. On Christmas Eve. For real. That's pretty magical.'

'Yes, it is.' There was a pause. I was thinking about last Christmas Eve, and I wondered if he was too. 'It would have been super magical if it had snowed last Christmas Eve.'

'I think it was magical anyway. And we wouldn't have seen the stars.' His voice was soft, and my knees started to turn to jelly. 'Do you want to walk? It's getting a bit chilly.'

'Okay. Which way?'

He nodded towards the end of the towpath leading away from the village. 'That way.'

'Great.' We set off, close together, our arms almost touching but not quite. 'But if you're getting chilly, why were you hanging around the towpath?' I wanted to add, *and at that particular lamp post?* But I didn't.

'Why? Because I knew you'd come.' He looked down at me at the same time as I looked up at him; our eyes met and there was that fizzing again. I couldn't look away.

'I think I came because I knew you'd be here.' My voice was practically a whisper. And now I'd verbalised it, I knew that was the reason I'd found myself wandering down here.

'I was waiting ages.' His voice was wry.

'I think I'd almost frozen to the spot. Bloody glad you came when you did.'

'I'd hate to see you frozen. I don't think you'd suit being blue and immobile all over. But seriously, the village misses you, Sam. Are you going to get back to work soon? They all know vaguely what happened, and nobody blames you. You can't lurk around towpaths forever.'

He stopped and turned to me, and I stopped with him.

Now we were facing each other, and he took my hands in his and looked down at them. 'Cerys, we both know this isn't about giving me a pep talk to tell me to go back to work. I'm going back. I am. I'm going there tonight, with my head held high and all the hassle of the last few days behind me. I just wanted to get a few things sorted first, without the distractions of work. Or anyone speculating on what's going on.' He took a deep, shuddering breath. 'She's not coming back this time. I think the whole village has worked that one out. They don't know the reasons, and that's nobody's business. But I'll tell you because I owe it to you, and I want to tell you. I really do. Belinda and I — we both want very different things. It's never going to work between us again, and too much has happened anyway. Nobody really knows what goes on behind closed doors — all the arguments, or all the times where we didn't even speak . . . and that was somehow worse. But now. Now it's sorted. And it's well and truly over. We're not fooling anyone else any more, and we certainly aren't fooling ourselves.'

I wondered exactly how much she'd told him and was willing to bet it wasn't everything.

'Oh?' was all I said.

'Yes. 'Oh'. She says she wants to live and work in London. She told me that the more the months went by, the more she'd stopped feeling disappointed that she wasn't pregnant . . . in fact, it sounds like she was feeling more relieved that she wasn't. She said that it wasn't fair on me because she knows how much I want kids, and she's not entirely sure she does. Anyway, that was just the start of it. I asked if there was someone else, and she didn't deny it. Then she kind of implied that she may not necessarily want kids with me, but she's not ruling out a serious relationship with someone else in the future. Someone who is more suited to her new lifestyle. In fact, the friend she's going to stay with until she can boot that latest set of tenants out is called Guy. I saw some messages on her phone. Which makes me think she lied about that message last year as well. The one I showed you. I think she *did* want to break up, then thought she was pregnant and panicked.'

Oh, how close he was to the truth. But I knew I would never, ever tell him what that truth was. And, to be fair to Belinda, the story she had told him, the reasons behind the final break-up, were as close to the truth as I think she could have made it. Anything more and it would have brought my brother into disrepute as well, and I wasn't having him linked with Belinda. *No. That could stay as what it was*. A horrible mistake that I knew for sure Geraint wouldn't be repeating. I didn't like Belinda, and she didn't like me, but deep down I hoped she could find what she was looking for with someone else; it was just very sad that she'd kept up the pretence all these months. Maybe she hadn't really been sure about leaving Sam properly — maybe part of her did want to try and work things out, but the real truth of the matter was that they had simply fallen out of love and had both now acknowledged, and accepted, that it was time to go their separate ways.

So, I answered Sam's comments in the best, non-committal way I could: '*Err-ruuumphhhh*. . . ahhhh . . . yeeessssss . . .' Followed by a wisely sage nod.

To my surprise, Sam suddenly laughed. 'God, I love it when you fumble your words and make up noises when you don't quite know what to say. Oh — was that CD anything important, by the way? Sorry — I forgot to get it off you, didn't I? After all that kicked off. I do apologise.'

'No, no, it's fine. It was just some different music to try in the Spatchcock. That's all. My brother's demo disc. It's really good, actually. He's pretty talented.'

I made a mental note to either try and scrub the words 'Belinda's Confession' off the disc, or to just steal another one off Geraint.

'Great. I look forward to listening to it. But you know, like I said, I *do* love the way you fumble your words. I love the way you champion your brother. I love the way you keep Edie's feet on the ground. In fact —' He squeezed my hands even more tightly '— I think I could actually love . . . *you*. If you let me. If you'll forgive me for being an idiot all these months and not sorting this out sooner. I can't believe Belinda and I spent so long trying to patch up something so completely broken. I doubt you did it intentionally, but if you did — thank you for waiting, Cerys. Thank you for just being . . . you. For just being here tonight and listening to me.' Then he frowned again and looked away for a second, as if he was measuring his words and needed to think about how to say something quite difficult. 'You know, even if Belinda and I had been lucky enough to get pregnant, it would have come with its own set of problems. I can't see her wanting to stick around and be a mum. Using the baby as a designer accessory — yes. But actually being a mum, and caring for it and loving it? I can't see that happening in her life for quite some time. I think there's a lot more she wants to do before settling down properly — and I hope she finds someone to do it with. And I'm mad with myself that I didn't understand that sooner and just cut my losses last year. I'm so sorry, Cerys. I feel that's an entire year I've wasted — a year I could have maybe spent with you.' He looked away, and the expression on his face was pained. I realised it was probably a difficult thing to confess to, but then he took a deep breath and said more, in a low, urgent voice.

'In the future, you see, I would love to

spend Christmas with a girl who wears elf slippers and snowflake leggings and was prepared to eat Frosties and milk for Christmas lunch because her friend was in a bad place. I want to help her choose a name for her next potted Christmas tree. I want to learn more about that girl's music and why it took years for her to agree to perform live when it was the best live music the Spatchcock has ever had, and I want to tell her about how it makes people feel when she plays guitar and sings, and how she makes people feel in *general*, and how I'd travel all the way to London, or just down the road in Padcock, or anywhere else she happened to be, just to deliver her a Christmas lunch, just to see her smile. And I want to get her a snow machine so every year she can have the best ever Padcock Christmas Craft Fair.'

'*Paahhh . . . ummmmm . . . ergggh-hhh . . .*' I said, my voice petering out. He looked at me, and, despite the madness, the craziness of this whole situation, I could see there was a tentative smile threatening at the edge of his lips.

'What was that?' he teased. 'You *are* playing in the pub tonight? Excellent. We'd better get there and get set up, eh?'

'Oh, for God's sake!' I suddenly laughed and pulled him closer. 'Yes, you *know* I'll bloody play in the pub tonight. But only because it's you, and only because you made it snow for me, and only because — well — I *want* to. And Sam — I want to do *this* too. And I want to be that girl you were talking about. I so want that.' Then, to my surprise, I found myself standing on my tiptoes, pressing my lips against his, and his arms came around me and pulled me even closer, and we stayed there for a very long time indeed . . .

And, yes. Just in case you're wondering: this *is* a Christmas story — it's *my* Christmas story. And in the spirit of all good Christmas stories, yes, it began to snow. Properly. Without the aid of a snow machine.

And the church bells rang out for the Christmas Eve carol service.

And we turned around, our arms around one another, and we made our way back up the towpath towards Padcock. Towards the Spatchcock. Towards home.

And towards all our Christmases yet to come.

Because I knew, without a doubt and from the bottom of my heart, that there'd be absolutely shedloads . . .

Thank You

Thank you so much for reading, and hopefully enjoying, *Christmas of New Beginnings*. It's the first book in the 'Padcock' series and I loved introducing Cerys, Sam and Edie. I am already quite attached to this new location and its quirky collection of residents. I hope you'll join me for more books in this series, and that we find out more about Edie next time around!

However, authors need to know they are doing the right thing, and keeping our readers happy is a huge part of the job. So, it would be wonderful if you could find a moment just to write a quick review on the website where you bought this book to let me know that you enjoyed the story. Thank you once again, and do feel free to contact me at any time on Facebook, Twitter, through my website (details on the following page), or through my lovely publishers, Choc Lit.

Thanks again, and much love to you all,

Kirsty
xx

www.twitter.com/kirsty_ferry
http://www.facebook.com/kirsty.ferry.author/

We do hope that you have enjoyed reading this large print book.

Did you know that all of our titles are available for purchase?

We publish a wide range of high quality large print books including:
Romances, Mysteries, Classics General Fiction Non Fiction and Westerns

Special interest titles available in large print are:
The Little Oxford Dictionary Music Book, Song Book Hymn Book, Service Book

Also available from us courtesy of Oxford University Press:
Young Readers' Dictionary (large print edition) Young Readers' Thesaurus (large print edition)

For further information or a free brochure, please contact us at:
**Ulverscroft Large Print Books Ltd., The Green, Bradgate Road, Anstey, Leicester, LE7 7FU, England.
Tel:** (00 44) **0116 236 4325
Fax:** (00 44) **0116 234 0205**

A CHRISTMAS CONSPIRACY

Kate Finnemore

Painting conservator Grace is excited to be joining the Christmas celebrations at a rural French château, along with her dress-designer sister Natasha. She's looking forward to helping her sister put on a fashion show, studying the château's extensive collection of paintings, taking part in a murder mystery evening — and perhaps falling in love with her hostess's son, bad-boy singer-songwriter Kai Curtis. But events soon start to take a sinister turn . . .

FACE THE MUSIC

Jenny Worstall

Dazzlingly talented orchestral violinist Allegra is travelling to Spain for a concert tour when she bumps into the last person on earth she wants to see: her ex-fiancé Zack. But love might just find a way to give their relationship the second chance it so richly deserves! However, there will be plenty of drama — including a stolen violin, secrets from the past, mysterious photos and an unexploded World War Two bomb — before Allegra finds her happy ever after . . .